WHAT MAKES US ALIKE?

a novel

Donna Dias Manuel

ISBN 978-93-5438-579-7

First published in India 2021 by Leadstart Inkstate
A Division of One Point Six Technologies Pvt Ltd

119-123, 1st Floor, Building J2,B - Wing,
Wadala Truck Terminal, Wadala East,
Mumbai 400022, Maharashtra, INDIA
Phone: +91 969933000
Email: info@leadstartcorp.com
www.leadstartcorp.com

Disclaimer: The views expressed in this book are those of the Author and do not pertain to be held by the Publisher.

Editor: Cora Bhatia
Cover: Shrinivas Rao
Layouts: Kshitij Dhawale

Dedication

For my mother and daughter

ACKNOWLEDGEMENTS

My deepest gratitude to my readers – both of this novel and of the first. Your heart-warming reviews and generous words of encouragement instilled the confidence I needed to write this story.

A sincere thank-you to my husband, Nigel. Without you, I would have never published this novel. Thank you for putting up with me on days that I found it hard to step out of my characters' world. You tolerate all my idiosyncrasies, for that I am ever grateful.

To my daughter, Zara. You show me what it is to love unconditionally. When I look at myself through your eyes, I know I am blessed. You will always be my most beautiful creation. You are my rainbow, my hope. Thank you for believing in me.

My eternal thanks to my sister, Juderica Dias Khetarpaul. We've had several creative differences, but those long video calls and multiple rounds of editing and re-writing is what makes this creative weave so strong.

A huge shout-out to my early readers Natasha Dias Over and Valentina Pinto Pavri. You have helped shape some of the characters with your incomparable insights. Thank you.

To the wonderful team at Leadstart Publishing, my editor Cora, and Ananya, I couldn't have been in better hands. To the entire design and production team, thank you for bringing this book to life and for all the hard work you've put in on my behalf.

Finally, my heartfelt thanks to my mother, Rita. Even if the world gave up on me, I know you will always have my back. I love you!

Chapter One

17 May 2017

Washington, D.C., USA

'Mom,' Zasha thundered through the back door, throwing her gymsack plump with her sweaty soccer uniform and cleats by the kitchen island, zigzagging her way through the pile of unopened mail on the floor.

'Mom,' she hollered again, this time a pitch higher.

'I'm down here,' Eira's voice echoed from the basement.

Wednesdays, she worked from home, a perk TJ Ellipse Architects had recently implemented to give their employees some flexibility. Zasha hurried down the wooden stairs and pushed through half a dozen carton boxes that were blocking the entrance to her mother's home-office.

'Ah, there you go. All fixed.' Eira looked proudly at the new printer-fax-scanner combo machine she'd just hooked up all by herself. Her makeshift office was an underused part of the storeroom in her basement and was quite spartan with a drafting table that had adjustable storage, a 15" MacBook Pro and now a fax machine.

'What do you think, Zasha?' Eira asked, loading the fax tray with paper.

'We need to talk, mom.' Zasha interrupted her mother's triumphant moment.

'I want to know why you are hell-bent on embarrassing me! I've done the bastard child and then came close to becoming a prisoner's child, what next?' Zasha bellowed, looking her mother in the eye. At five feet two, she was now only an inch shorter than Eira.

'Hold that tongue right there,' Eira sputtered. 'What's bothering you?' Colour leached from her face that was now stamped with guilt and concern. Lately, she didn't know what to expect from Zasha. She could explode any time without warning.

'Are you really going to play the "dumb" card?' Zasha asked pointedly.

'Zip your potty mouth, young lady. I've had enough of your verbal diarrhoea, for two years now.' Eira admonished, staring her preteen daughter down with authority. 'This is not you. This is all Mia.'

Eira felt her ears go red. She was exasperated by her daughter's disregard for her. They'd been the Gilmore Girls; they were best friends before mother and daughter. But then Shikhar came along, and before she knew it, Zasha was in love with him. Eira knew that if there was ever going to be a father in her daughter's life, it had to be Shikhar. He loved Eira and treated her right, but more importantly, he loved Zasha, and Zasha loved him, too. How was she supposed to know he'd turn her daughter against her, or for that matter land himself in prison!

'Great, just great. Now blame my best friend for all your madness.' Zasha let out a bitter laugh. 'Mia is the only one who gets me. Thanks to her, I've survived Shikhar going to prison. So please, don't drag her into this conversation.'

'Here we go again. Somehow, I seem to ace at being the disappointing parent, don't I? Mia's mother seems to have it all together with her pretty bakes and excellent carpooling service.' Eira was clearly in no mood to let this one go.

'You sound silly Mom. But we're not talking about Mia's mother right now. We're talking about you and Dr Zane. Mia and her mother saw you'll leisurely enjoying a coffee outside the hospital, and he wasn't in his scrubs or wearing that geeky white doctor coat of his, so don't tell me you just happened to bump into him.'

'And what did you infer from their observation?' Eira's eyebrows knitted in frustration.

'That you guys are at it!' Zasha's face creased.

'Zasha, Stop it!'

'You asked what I thought, isn't that what's going on? Mia saw him hold your hand, and she even described the pathetic love-sick look on his face.'

'I umm...well we...' Eira stuttered, the words twirling in her mouth.

'Save it. I'll be thirteen in just about seven months. I've never been on a date, but I'm not dumb.' Zasha rolled her eyes. 'Your secret's out, but I've handled it.'

'Let me ex...ppp...l...' Eira's anger departed abruptly. 'Sorry, what do you mean by you've handled it?'

'I gave her a reasonable explanation. I told Mia that Dr Zane's been pestering you to go out with him and that you pitied the guy, so you went out with him this one time and that I knew all about it.' Intercepting the look of fear on Eira's face, Zasha's deep-set brown eyes that she had inherited from her mother, lit up with a smug sense of satisfaction.

'Now that's just wrong on so many counts, Zasha. Why would you do that?'

'Because this is such hogwash. I don't want a patchwork family. I want a dad who's present in my life every day or just no dad at all. No more revolving door! I was happy Mom, have you forgotten? I wanted you and Shikhar to be together. I thought we were going to be a family. But you abandoned him when he needed you the most and sent him packing to prison.' Zasha rattled off. 'You should be the one serving prison time, not him!' She squawked.

'Go to your room, now!' Eira glowered. Zasha's words had sliced her heart in two. She never missed an opportunity to blame Eira for Shikhar's prison sentence. Zasha simply refused to believe he could do any wrong.

'Great parenting, Mom.' Zasha smirked. 'The only reason Nani does not say anything is because...never mind. I'm pretty sure she agrees with me too.'

'You leave Nani alone,' Eira warned, turning away to hide her tears. Zasha's acerbic remarks jabbed her already bleeding heart like rusty pins.

Later that evening, after finishing the last edits on her presentation, Eira poured herself a glass of chilled Prosecco and settled on the couch with her iPad. Netflix and wine were great mood fixers. She scrolled through the shows that were last watched; there was Aziz Ansari, Russell Peters and Vir Das too. *The Cats were definitely watching TV together*, Eira thought to herself and smiled wryly. *The Cats* that's what she called her mother and daughter, who had become quite a team in the last twenty-four months. And just as she was about to scroll down further, she noticed something. There it was – *13 Reasons Why*. Eira had explicitly told her mother that Zasha wasn't allowed to watch this suicide-based American teen show no matter how hard she pressed. Why then was it showing up on the last-watched-shows scroll bar? *Was Zasha watching this show? What's cooking in her brain? Should I talk to the school counsellor or let this roll over?* Eira's brain was flooded with questions about her daughter's growing indiscretions. Zasha's behaviour was getting out of hand; she had to be checked before it was too late. Eira decided to have the disciplinary chat with Zasha once again and soon.

Propping a cushion under her aching feet for support, Eira punched in Nikki's digits. If there was anyone who could help her out of this mess it had to be her best friend; besides, she was Zasha's paternal aunt, too.

'Hi, Nikki.'

'Hey, babe. This is a late call. All okay?' Nikki asked, struggling to hold the phone between her ear and shoulder as she rummaged through her closet for her PJs.

'I'm up shit creek without a paddle.'

'What happened?' Nikki cleared her throat. She had just finished her daily salt-water gargle ritual and was getting ready for bed. 'Are Zasha and Kanika aunty alright?'

'Yes, they are fine and in bed. At least my mother is…Zasha must be piercing the voodoo doll she's made of me.'

'Ha ha, what did our little Diva do now?'

'Firstly, she's no longer a little girl. That angel left this house two years ago. Secondly, she's a complete drama queen. With her, you can never tell when a perfectly peaceful conversation will turn into a rage-filled diatribe. There are moments I want to smack her hard.'

'Now, now. You don't want her calling child services, do you?'

'Maybe she should call them and spend some time in foster care.'

'This sounds serious. Spill it.'

'You should hear how she speaks to me. Shikhar's presence is similar to a ghost's in this house. He just won't leave us in peace. Zasha told me that I should be in prison instead of him. She thinks he deserves a better life than her own mother does. I drive myself insane working a crushing seventy-hour week, and she wants *me* to go to prison.'

'Okay, please take a deep breath. We don't want you in the emergency room. You're going to give yourself a stroke like this. Please sip some water,' Nikki urged.

Eira sipped her white wine instead letting the fizzy, sweet liquid swirl around her tongue.

'I know I shouldn't have listened to her. I shouldn't be going out on dates anymore. I'm going to die single.'

'Huh. Who's her and what dates? You didn't tell me you were dating again,' Nikki asked quizzically.

'Alice, my crazy colleague, advised me that age wasn't going to be on my side for much longer, and so I shouldn't be holed up and get out more frequently.' Eira sighed. 'Well, Z found out, and it led to a showdown this afternoon. I have such rotten luck.'

'So, here's the thing, Alice is *not* who you should go to for love advice. That's what I'm here for. Next, is there potential with this mystery man?'

'There's *lots* of potential, but he's different,' Eira said dreamy-eyed.

'Different. How?'

'Nihal is kind and funny, drives a Kia Sorento, and he likes picnics.'

'I'm not sure about the picnics, but the rest sounds perfectly normal to me.'

'Wait, here comes the weirdest part; he likes talking about his work even when I'm not asking. He loves yapping about his cases. I know the names of all his interns, the resident doctors, the other attending doctors, and some nurses too. Did I mention he is an attending paediatric surgeon at GW University Hospital?'

'Okay. So that first part was shallow. I like Kia cars.'

'Me too. I wasn't poking fun at his car. It's not as if I drive a Porsche. It's just that I've never dated a man who isn't crazy about his wheels, and I know he makes pots of money. Surgeons rake in the moolah. But he is so—'

'Humble? Not flashy? Good, right?'

'Kinda.' Eira stared at her fingers: they were long and bony with an odd deep green vein bulging along the back of her hand.

'Hmm. As far as talking about his work goes…isn't that what most women want? A man who shares his day and asks about hers too.'

'Yea, I guess. But Shikhar never spoke about work, leave alone ask about what I did all day. His day was always good, busy, boring or tiring. One-word answers. Nothing to explain the good or the boring parts.'

'And look where that ended. Shikhar is not the best person to compare your doctor with, since he turned out to be a man with many secrets and dragged you into his mess too. I liked Shikhar, but I don't care much for his cool attitude anymore.'

'Pfft. I know—'

'Just take it slow and stop overanalysing. How long have you two been dating? One…two months.'

'Five actually.'

'What? You've kept this from me for five months?'

'Five months just *sounds* long. It's not as if we go out every day. He's on call at the hospital, and of course, with me trying to pick the best time when I won't get interrogated by my daughter, I land up making these complicated colour coded excel sheets. I send them to him to see if he can schedule a date using my sheets, and it turns out our schedules rarely match. So, we must make do with texting like teenagers or grabbing a bite at a coffee shop close to the hospital, which is when you get caught by your daughter's best friend, who insists your boyfriend has a love-sick puppy look on his face!' Eira exhaled a defeated breath.

'Sounds like a regular single mom's life to me.'

'It's a little too normal, and you know I don't like regular.'

'Age my love, makes the ordinary seem extraordinary,' Nikki chuckled.

'I don't like hiding. I *don't* know why I lied to Zasha in the first place. I'm the mother and I am—' Eira felt a hot tear slide down her cheek.

'Babe, you're doing your best to give her a stable life,' Nikki reasoned. 'Zasha is on the cusp of becoming a teenager. She's just acting out like most teens; they rebel and try to be as difficult as possible. Hormones! We were mercurial at that age too. Remember?' Nikki pointed, climbing into bed.

'I didn't have the nerve to speak to my mother the way she does, for sure.'

'I know, honey. But times have changed, and you were the one who taught her to talk about her feelings, right from the time she was a toddler.' Nikki reminded, fluffing her pillow.

'Yea, it's come back to bite me in the ass. Anyway, I've decided to lay low for a few days, and see how it goes. I know I can't avoid the topic by sending her to her room, but for now, I don't want any drama. I'm snowed under with work at the office; it's going to be an intense two weeks, and if it all goes well, I will finally get that promotion I've been working so hard for.'

'I really hope you get the promotion, but I'm not done with this conversation. So how come I didn't know anything about this Dr Nihal and his moves?'

'Nikki, you know how my relationship with Shikhar blew up in my face. I'm still so embarrassed about how I didn't see it coming. I didn't feel ready to tell the world I'm dating again, and as I shared, Zane is different. I don't even know if it will last, then why talk about him until I'm sure.'

'Question. Is his name Nihal or Zane, you're confusing me.'

'Nihal Zane. But he's used to being addressed by his last name, so he doesn't mind either one.' Just saying his name out aloud made her tingle. A warm, bubbly feeling fizzed inside her.

'Are you smiling to yourself?' Nikki teased.

'No. Why would I be smiling?' Eira flushed, growing defensive. 'At the rate things are going, I may have to start attending funerals.'

'Huh?'

'You know what they say, in your twenties weddings are hunting grounds for singles. In your thirties, funerals are a better bet,' Eira said sagely.

'You just made that up.' Nikki laughed. 'So, have you and Nihal eaten dessert or you guys crawling slow?'

'With teenzilla stomping around the house demanding we don't see each other, I doubt I'll ever see the insides of a man again.'

'Insides of a man,' Nikki parroted. 'You're funny. I like that term. I'm gonna ask my husband to show me his insides tonight.' Nikki tittered. 'Gnite girl. Sleep it off, and remember, I have your back, always, okay?'

'Okay, Hon. Thanks for not giving me the third degree and just letting me vent. I love you. Good Night.'

Eira clicked her phone off and set it down on the table. She drained the rest of her drink in the sink and looked up at the wall clock; it was 11 p.m. Nihal would still be at work. Acting on impulse, Eira quickly tiptoed to her room and wiped away the generously spread night cream off her face. Standing before her open closet, she contemplated wearing her polka dotted, cross back summer dress that still had the tag on, but that would scream, "I dressed up especially for you." Finally, she went with a more casual look. Eira pulled on a pair of distressed, white, skinny jeans that accentuated her perfect derrière, but she had to suck in her baby pouch to zip up. She had gained forty pounds during her pregnancy but lost most of it in the first year itself; the last four strong-willed ones she carried around ever since, as a mommy badge of honour. There was a nip in the air that night, so she threw on a light V-neck black sweater and looped a mint-coloured infinity scarf around her neck. Eira slapped on a little mascara making her pecan shaped brown eyes pop. She dabbed a generous amount of gloss on her full lips before running her fingers through her recently touched up auburn-coloured highlights and twisted it into a casual top knot bun. This was Eira being adventurous; she was stepping out of her scheduled love life and living in the moment. She wanted to see Nihal. She wanted to feel his warm lips over hers before the next sunrise.

Chapter Two

'Hey. You busy?' Eira asked, attempting her usual casualness as if she was just in the neighbourhood.

'Hi, babe,' Nihal replied, his voice preoccupied. 'Let me call you back in two minutes.' Before she could say yes, he'd hung up on her.

Eira felt a little let down. She thought he'd sound all jumpy for her, as if he was only waiting to attend to her call. On the contrary, he wasn't even the least bit interested to know why she'd called so late.

I'm so stupid. Eira mumbled to herself. *What was I thinking, driving up to the hospital without checking with him first!* Eira slid her key back into the ignition when her cell phone launched into its hip-hop tune, a ringtone Zasha had saved on her phone. It was Nihal calling back like he said he would. This man was no mystery. He didn't play games. He spoke and acted just the way he felt. Eira accepted his call; it was the only thing to do. She was a thirty-four-year-old single mother, who didn't have the time or the energy to engage in a pointless cat and mouse chase.

'Eira. Sorry about that earlier. I just wanted to be done with some pending paperwork and leave. It's been a long *long* day,' Nihal said, swiping his employee ID card to punch out for the day.

'No problem. You head home and get a good night's rest.' Eira rolled up her window so he wouldn't hear passing cars. She didn't want him to know she was in the parking lot of the hospital. But as fate would have it, the car alarm of an old Toyota parked eight slots away began to beep.

Why? Why? Why? She muttered to herself, hoping he didn't hear the alarm go off.

'Eira, where are you?' He asked. Of course, he knew she was always in bed by eleven and up by six every morning. He'd seen her schedule. Nothing changed. Seven hours of sleep was a must. Clearly, she wasn't home like she said she would be when they spoke earlier in the day.

'Umm. Out,' Eira replied. 'Actually, I'm in the parking lot.'

'You went back to work?'

'No. The hospital parking lot,' she replied sheepishly.

'Hospital? What happened? Who's in the hospital? Do you need me to come over?'

'I'm in your hospital parking lot, dummy,' Eira replied, nearly eating up the *"your"* in that sentence.

'Why?' He paused, and then lowering his voice to a whisper, he asked, 'Did you come to surprise me?'

'I wanted to see you.' Eira's cheeks flushed.

'Which floor are you parked on? Let me come to you.' She heard him smile.

'I'm on 3A.' Eira's heart was galloping like a racehorse inside her rib cage. She wanted him in her life. She didn't want to say goodbye. Not yet. This couldn't be their last meeting. She would have to make Zasha understand, but convincing Zasha wasn't going to be easy. She needed help. Nikki could be of *some* assistance, but she had to bring in the big guns. The Cats were a close-knit team now. Eira decided to exploit the situation and get her mother to talk sense into Zasha.

But of course, she didn't want to take her mother's help. Eira prided herself on having an unshakeable relationship with her daughter, but in the last two years, it had all gone horribly wrong.

How do I ask Mummy for her help? She will gloat at my misery and give me an hour-long lecture about Zasha being a chip off the old block. God! How I'm going to hate having that conversation.

'Eira,' Nihal knocked on the passenger side door of her Mini Cooper, jerking her out of her thoughts.

'Hey, beautiful.' Nihal kissed her softly on her cheek. He breathed in the scent of her skin – she smelled like fresh spring. 'I *love* the surprise. I honestly didn't think this day would end so well.' He flashed a dimpled smile. Nihal had been on call for thirty-two hours, but in his line of work, such long shifts weren't out of the ordinary. There was never a dull moment in the OR.

Eira couldn't take her eyes off him; even in the dimly lit parking lot, he looked gorgeous in his blue, button down collar shirt. The gently tapered sleeves highlighted his athletic body. He was wearing his favourite Spider-Man cufflinks. Nihal had dump truck and troll shaped cufflinks too. The kids loved it; back in the day, Zasha loved them too. Eira loved his understated sense of dressing. Minus the cufflinks, his wardrobe stayed the same – white shirts, blue shirts, white shirts with blue stripes, blue shirts with white stripes and once, just that one time she'd seen him in a black casual shirt. But given that they always met in or around the hospital during work hours, she didn't know how he dressed on weekends.

This was the first time Eira was dating a man who wasn't an Indian. Technically, he did have Indian roots. His maternal grandparents were of Indian origin, but he was of mixed heritage: an African-American father and an Indian origin, South African mother. Nihal had adorable curls and olive skin, and he towered over her at six-feet-two.

'I'm glad you love the surprise.' Eira gave his palm a little squeeze, slowly entwining her fingers with his. The fear of losing him made her desire for him even stronger. She unbuckled her seatbelt, turned towards him and kissed him hard. Her lips grazed the sides of his mouth, and his day-old stubble tickled her skin. The musky smell of his masculinity made her heart quicken. His mouth was now slowly moving down her neck closer to her collarbone, and every muscle in her body ached with raw desire.

Buzz. Buzz.

Eira's eyes snapped open. Nihal's phone was vibrating in his bag.

'I have to take that,' Nihal pulled away from her abruptly. One of the resident doctors was calling to discuss a case file. When Nihal got off the call, Eira was buckled in, with her steering arm clenching the wheel.

'You're full of surprises,' Nihal said, trying to bring her face closer to his.

'I think I should head home. It's almost 11.40.'

'I'm sorry. I know we were in the middle of all that…but I had to take that call. Come on, don't be like this. Come home with me. I have the day off tomorrow.'

'But I have to go to work Nihal. I don't have the day off.' Eira sighed.

'I know, but just for a little bit. I love what we were—'

'No.' Eira stopped him mid-sentence. 'You don't understand. I'm a single mother. I can't just spend the night out like this.'

'I'm very aware that you're a single mom, Eira. I just thought we were being adventurous for once and not on a pre-planned schedule. I wasn't asking you to sleep over. I get it!'

'I'm sorry. I didn't mean it like that. I've got a lot going on at work, and home and Zasha's not making it any easier for me.' Eira omitted the volcanic episode with her daughter. She didn't want him to know Zasha had given her an ultimatum of sorts. 'You should go home. I'll call you tomorrow and try and see if we can do something together this weekend, if you're free that is.'

'You know I'm free on Saturdays, and you also know you will never be able to get out of your house unless you tell them the truth. Don't stress it Eira. I understand your situation, I really do.' He patted her hand lightly and left.

Eira drove home filled with regret. She rued bringing up the single-mother bit, but it was her life's truth, and she had to be in control. She couldn't afford to be impulsive no matter how liberating it felt. The last time she was impulsive, she fell pregnant.

Sixteen years ago, Eira and her mother moved from New Delhi to New York. Kanika's decision had been the talk of Chittaranjan Park's Bengali community. She took up an internal job posting with the United Nations and moved to the Big Apple with her daughter, while Eira's father chose to stay back in India. *Time Square doesn't make me tick. I'm not enamoured by its glitz and glam*, he'd say. Kanika knew she would be wasting her time trying to convince him to go with them. It's not as if he couldn't work on his paintings in Brooklyn. He'd made his choice and was sticking with it. It was time for her daughter to shine. Eira was smart as a whip, and with the right opportunity, Kanika believed she would go places. Eira had secured a spot at the prestigious Cornell University and Kanika was excited about her daughter's future.

Eira parked her car on the street. If she parked in the garage, she'd have to use the side door to enter the house, and that door squeaked like a mouse being chased for his life. She didn't want to wake the Cats up. As Eira slid her key through the front door, she noticed a faint yellow glow through the curtains; her reading light in the living room was switched on.

Mama Cat was awake.

She smelt blood.

Eira took a deep breath and entered the house. *Chin up. Chin up.* She encouraged herself. She couldn't avoid her mother; she had to pass the living room to get to the stairs to her bedroom.

'Hey, did I wake you?' Eira pretended to ask from concern.

'No. I couldn't sleep. I came down to get a glass of water, and then I heard your car drive off. So, I waited.' Kanika replied, adjusting the teal-coloured bookmark placed inside her book.

'Oh ok.'

'Good night, Eira. I'm going to bed now. I have my diabetes test tomorrow morning.'

'I can drop you to your appointment.' Eira offered.

'Thanks, but I'll take the metro. It will be faster.' Kanika picked up her reading glasses and made her way to the stairs leading to their bedrooms.

'Gnite, Mummy.' Eira couldn't believe it. Her mother wasn't asking leading questions. She'd watched her daughter drive away at 11 p.m. and return an hour later and still didn't ask about her whereabouts. This was atypical of her mother. Something inestimable was going to happen. All havoc was going to break loose the next morning.

'Mummy, one more thing, were you watching that show, *13 Reasons Why*, on my iPad?'

'Yea, I wanted to see what the fuss was all about. Everyone is talking about it on the internet, so I watched two episodes.' Kanika squinted. 'Did you think I let Zasha watch it?'

'Yes…No, I mean I thought she…' Eira stammered. She knew her mother would hate her guts.

'I follow the rules, Eira. I do my best to stick to the list you've put up on that fridge door, that's all a grandmother can do. See you in the morning.'

I follow the rules! Her mother had gone for the slow stab. Kanika was indirectly calling her a hypocrite. Eira had laid down new house rules post the Shikhar episode.

Rule No. 1 – Honest clear communication. *If you got to hide it, it's worth losing it.*

And here she was, sneaking behind her mother and daughter's back. There was no real need to hide Nihal, and yet she was doing just that.

Chapter Three

'You're up on time.' Kanika greeted Eira the next morning with a plate of steamed idlis.

'Morning, Mummy.' Eira yawned, perching herself on a kitchen stool. 'These look good.' Eira cut into a fluffy, disc shaped idli and placed a piece in her mouth. She was trying to make up for the previous night by being more appreciative of the person who was helping her raise her child.

'Mummy, about last night, I want to talk to you about something. I—'

'Coffee anyone?' Zasha skipped into the kitchen in a bright and perky mood

'Since when did you start drinking coffee?' Eira inhaled heavily.

'Since I had my first sip with Mia and the girls at The Rooster Café, a couple of weeks ago.'

'I didn't know about this,' Kanika threw her hands up in the air, 'before you ask me about her new coffee drinking routine.' She rolled her eyes and left the kitchen.

'No biggie, Mom. It's not as if I'm drinking alcohol. Kids my age have an Instagram profile and are busy posting absurd photos of themselves. This is just coffee.' Zasha said, pouring the ground coffee into the French press.

'Keep it to one a day. Too much coffee can make you jumpy.' Eira knew she had to let the alcohol comment slide. Her daughter was simply trying to work her up. Zasha was a smart kid; she had her head screwed on straight. She wouldn't get involved in drinking alcohol or smoking pot. But Zasha was at the threshold of teenage life. She was bound to want to experiment with the forbidden apple. She was growing up and she was going to make her own choices. Good choices and poor ones. Eira could no longer insulate her daughter from the outside world. She had already begun drinking coffee, what next? Boys?

No way.

She was too young for boyfriends. But Eira had her first crush at fifteen. It was quite possible her daughter could already be crushing on boys or girls for that matter. A month ago, while they were getting themselves a French manicure during their lunch break, Alice had told Eira all about the teenage dating apps. Absurd fears had been floating around in Eira's head ever since, making her mind go into overdrive. She had to stop talking to Alice about her life. But Eira couldn't rule out the possibility that her daughter could go down that road. She had to be more involved in Zasha's life. She had to make things right between them before it was too late, before their relationship became like the one she shared with her own mother.

'See you, Mom. My bus will be here any minute.' Zasha poured her coffee in a small travel mug and stuffed an idli into her mouth before running out the kitchen door. No hugs. No kisses. This was a sneak peek of the upcoming teenage years.

Kanika returned to pick her packed breakfast – a box of fruit and unsweetened yogurt and saw Eira staring blankly through the kitchen window.

'Eira, does your offer to drop me off for my appointment still hold good?'

'Sure. Let me get dressed for work and we can leave in fifteen minutes.' Eira confirmed. Kanika recognized the lost gaze she saw in her daughter's eyes. The confusion, the exhaustion, the desire, she'd experienced all of it too.

'Have you carried your health insurance card?' Eira double checked with Kanika before locking the car doors.

'Yes. I never take it out of my purse.'

Eira's office was a twenty-minute drive from home. She was glad she lived in D.C. and worked just across the Potomac River. This way, she avoided the rush hour traffic, and Zasha didn't have to travel too far to get to school. Three years ago, when they moved from New York to D.C. Eira knew that she'd have to avoid the suburban life. Zasha would never be able to adapt to a sprawling stone house with a giant oak tree in their front lawn and children playing in the backyard across the fence. She'd grown up in a two-bedroom apartment in Manhattan, which felt more like a single bedroom with some storage space thrown in as a makeshift toddler playroom. But they loved their cosy home. It was filled with memories; the ones they'd made together right from the time she first went to school. They'd lived in the same apartment for four years. The first year, on Zasha's sixth birthday, Eira went overboard and invited fifteen people to her birthday party. With three layers of a Dr Seuss cake occupying nearly half the dining table, and bowls of cheese puffs occupying the other half, Eira knew she had messed up the guest list. Their living room could accommodate six human beings at a time if they were to breathe in the oxygen in the room simultaneously. Kanika took a quick call and moved some furniture around and threw open the makeshift bedroom for the kids to go crazy. It was tight. But this was one of Zasha's favourite memories, and she spoke about it fondly every once in a while.

'Eira, do you want to tell me what's bothering you?' Kanika asked with caution. She had counselled Nikki on several occasions, but Eira rarely ever went to her mother for advice, not as a teenager, nor as a young adult who'd gotten herself pregnant out of wedlock, and definitely not as a mother. It was obvious to Kanika that Eira wanted to be radically different from her. But she was Eira's mother, and so she did what mothers do. Ask.

'I do. I've been meaning to talk to you about something.' Eira replied with a crease of worry on her brow. This was a surprise for Kanika. Eira had considered talking to her mother about her issues without an inch of probing.

'Go ahead. I'm listening.'

'Mummy, it's going to sound odd, but I'd like you to keep an open mind and try and consider my situation.'

'OK.'

'Well, I have been seeing a guy, for about five months now, and I didn't bring it up earlier because I was unsure about where it was going, but then Zasha got to know about it, and she is upset with me.'

'And you need my help.' Kanika concluded.

'Yes, in a way,' Eira swallowed.

'Is that where you were last night, with him?' Kanika asked pointedly.

'Yes.' Eira nodded. 'I don't know what got into me; I just had to go see him. It was late, and I didn't want to wake you up, so I left without informing you. Sorry. I know it was not a responsible thing to do.'

'Do you love him?' Kanika shut her eyes and held on to her seat piercing her nails into the soft leather. She couldn't bear to watch her daughter change lanes without signalling. Eira had never been in a car accident, but she had many close shaves. 'That wasn't very responsible either. You could have hit that car's bumper. Did you do that on purpose?' Kanika bleated.

'On purpose? No, don't be silly. That's how I drive. Always driven.'

'Please don't teach your daughter how to drive. One reckless person is more than enough in the family.'

'Okay, Mother. Chill. Won't happen again.'

'So, do you love him?' Kanika returned.

'I don't know if I love him. I am very fond of him.'

'He's not your pet. Fond is an odd word to use for a man you've been seeing for five months.'

'Like, fond, synonyms Mummy.' Eira chuckled, trying to make light of the moment.

'Let me rephrase, have either one of you said the words out loud?'

'No. It's too soon.' It had been thirteen years since Eira had such a specific conversation about love and relationships with her mother. The first and only time they spoke about love and marriage was the night Eira told her mother she was seven weeks pregnant and was keeping the baby. Eira had made it clear she didn't want any marital advice from her mother, who she felt had lived a marriage of convenience. So, what was different this time between Nihal and her that she needed her mother's intervention?

'There's no right or wrong time to say, "I love you" if you feel it. If love exists, you say it. If it doesn't, then you don't.'

'I want to continue seeing him and see where it goes.' Eira continued, a little uncomfortable with the direct talk.

'And Zasha has given you an ultimatum?' Kanika prodded.

'In a way. She threw a fit yesterday and brought up Shikhar; she just won't let it go! Mia has been filling her ears.'

'Mia is good for Zasha. Initially, I was worried about that girl, but I've seen them together, she's not trouble. Her dressing is borderline goat, but...'

'Goth,' Eira interrupted her lips parting in a half-smile. Her mother's pronunciations were always amusing.

'Yes, Goth.' Kanika continued unaffected. 'Mia may have shared her observation in good faith, but you know Zasha has a flair for the dramatics. Let her cool down. You take your time and figure out what it is you and this man want.'

'You mean define our relationship. But why is that important?'

'Call me old school, but if you're going to introduce him to your daughter, you will need a definition. It's time you work on that first.' Kanika remarked. 'What is his name?'

'Nihal Zane.'

'African?' Kanika raised an eyebrow.

'African-American and Indian too.'

'Black, *black* African?'

'Are we really doing this?' Eira asked, turning left at the corner. They'd made it to the appointment ten minutes early.

'I want to know.'

'He is lighter than me, if that's your question.' Eira teased. 'We're Bengali, Mom, not the fairest bunch in the Indian community.'

'I wasn't trying to be racist. I just wanted to know his background.'

'Aah, hence the emphasis on black?' Eira's eyes were a-sparkle.

'You're twisting my words.' Kanika nodded in defeat.

'So, are you cool with it?' Eira licked her lips with the hope she'd see an approving nod.

'We're not done here. I'm not committing to anything until you give me more information—his age, marital status, family information, professional goals. I want all the details. If you want me to back you, I need to be sure Zasha is going to be alright this time.' Kanika leaned forward to pick up her paisley printed bag lying at her foot.

'Nihal is a paediatric—'

'Stop.' Kanika's brow furrowed. 'We're not doing this in the car. This is not a parking lot conversation, Eira. Let's sit down at home and have a proper chat. What's the hurry? And yes, I'd like to meet him first before I play cheerleader.'

She unbuckled her seatbelt and peeped through the glass window to make sure it was safe to get out. 'I'll see you at home. Thanks for the drop, and please drive safe.'

Eira watched her mother cautiously step on to the sidewalk clutching her breakfast box, while her Vera Bradley tote gently bumped against her side. Kanika was physically slower than she used to be just three years earlier, but retirement had added a lot more colour to her life. Her time was now her own, and she could spend it on projects that were dear to her heart. Kanika was President of the South Asian Women's Welfare Centre and treasurer of the Green Feet movement started a year ago by a group of enthusiastic University students. She was also part of Fanny's book club, a women's-only book club that every booklover wanted to be a member of. But entry to this senior citizen sorority was by invite only. Kanika was thrilled that she didn't have to pull any strings; Fanny herself had written to invite Kanika to join them.

Eira had always known her mother to be on the ball. In her illustrious career, spanning three and a half decades she'd never once seen her mother whine about the craziness of balancing a career and a home. She made sure she was present at every inter-school debate and cheered the loudest at her sports day events, even when Eira was performing at her worst. Kanika sat in the front row for all school performances, just so she'd get good printable photographs for her special *Eira's Wonder Years* album. Packed lunches were a must. No cafeteria food. Even when she travelled for work, she'd draw up a list of Eira's favourite dishes and make Pinky Mashi, the nanny, practice the recipes on the weekend before she left. Pinky Mashi was her mother's most trusted aide. It took Kanika a good while to get around the fact that her granddaughter would be eating her lunches at school.

It was all rainbows and unicorns between mother and daughter, until one fateful Diwali *taash* party, Brinda *Kaki*, Eira's paternal aunt, unmindful of her loud voice after consuming three glasses of rum and cola decided to applaud Kanika for her brilliant parenting.

'Look at you, Kanika, I don't know how you do it all – the school stuff, work, home. Eira is a handful now. From not wanting kids and crying for weeks about your pregnancy, you're a super mom now. Does *bhai* pitch in at all or is he sticking to his *I didn't want a child spiel*?' Brinda Kaki asked innocently, as she chewed on sweet paan. Her high-pitched, nasal voice seeped from under the heavy door. She was unaware that eleven-year-old Eira, who was trying to climb up the wooden bureau outside the bedroom to reach her Scrabble box perched on the steel *almari* had overheard their conversation. Eira stood still for the next six minutes unable to hear anything else, but her racing heartbeat that was now louder than the Rajdhani Express making its way into New Delhi's Ajmeri gate station. She felt her heart slowly detach from her body, and the love she had for her mother drain from it. Her little heart had been punctured by the ugly truth that she was a mistake – an unwanted child.

Eira spent her teenage years despising her mother; although, unlike Zasha she never spoke about it openly. Only when Zasha was born the ice between them began to thaw. In a way, life had come full circle for Eira, only this time she was at the receiving end.

Chapter Four

Whatsapp Chat

Nikki: So, I Facebooked your Dr Zane.

Eira: Noun. Facebook is a noun. And why are you stalking him?

Nikki: You sprung one on me last night, and you think I wouldn't look him up?

Eira: I haven't added him on FB yet.

Nikki: What? How are you doing your background check?

Eira: I have you for that ☺

Nikki: Seriously?

Eira: Yup. I don't have time for all this social media jazz. I barely get my legs waxed. Besides, if anyone should hide something, they're not going to put it up on FB for the world to see.

Nikki: Agree to disagree. Anyway, he's hot.

Eira: You think?

Nikki: I'm happily married, but I can tell hot. He's a cross between a Will Smith and Trevor Noah. And I like how last night you skipped mentioning he's African-American. I won't deny your choice in men surprises me.

Eira: I didn't skip mentioning his race; we just didn't get to the whole description part. Oh, and there's a sprinkle of Indian in him too. And btw, you sound like my mother. She called him black!

Nikki: Ha ha you told her? Wow, giant step taken.

Eira: I did it this morning, and she wants to "chat" about it when I get home ☹ SAVE Me.

Nikki: She might be able to help with Zasha.

Eira: Why do you think I told her!

Nikki: Smart girl. So, when am I going to meet the doctor?

Eira: After I get some time with him.

Nikki: I can fly down next weekend if you guys are free. I haven't seen my only niece in three months.

Eira: Don't you dare get on that plane. I must deal with Zasha first and my mother wants to meet him too.

Nikki: Oh cool. So, I can come when you invite him over to meet Kanika aunty.

Eira: No way. I don't want him to feel as if he's being interrogated by my mother, daughter, and best friend. Besides, I haven't asked him yet. I don't know if he'll agree. It's too soon. Don't you think?

Nikki: If you were a 21 yo I'd say too soon, but he knows you have a daughter and that your mother lives with you. I don't really think it's too soon.

Eira: He's a bit miffed with me right now. After you and I spoke last night, I did something stupid.

Nikki: Didn't you say you were going to bed after we hung up?

Eira: Well, I didn't. I drove to the hospital to see him and then acted like a hormonal teenager and kissed him in the parking lot. And when he had to take a work call in the middle of our make-out session, I got all pissed off and refused to go home with him by making it doubly clear that I was a single mother who didn't have time for sex and romance. Kill me now.

Nikki: You really did that? The first part. Act on impulse. I am so proud of you. Finally!

Eira: Did you read my entire text?

Nikki: Yes. That is typical Eira, so I'm not surprised. Make it up to him. Go surprise him at lunch today.

Eira: Are you nuts? I'm at work.

Nikki: Well, if his FB profile is any indicator of his social life, he has a few good-looking female friends. Of course, he hasn't added any photos, just tagged in them. Seems as if he isn't a regular user either.

Eira: He's a surgeon...busy saving lives.

Nikki: Well, your surgeon has plenty of time to barbecue and go fly fishing ☺ . A surgeon with things other than a scalpel in his hand is good.

Nikki: I miss you. Days like this, I wish we lived closer.

Eira: I offered to hop on a flight, remember? I could always do with a liquid lunch with my favourite girl.

Eira: Fat chance. You stay put. NO surprises. Gotta go. Gina is giving me the how-much-longer glare.

Nikki: Who's Gina?

Eira: My boss, you idiot. Bye now.

Nikki: No wait.

Eira: Bye.

Eira returned to her laptop screen and saw three messages from Gina on the office messenger. *So, I spent a little time chatting on my phone, at least, I'm not wasting the rest of the day scrolling through Facebook or posting selfies taken in the office loo on Instagram,* Eira convinced herself. *Gina has to give me a break.*

Eira had worked at TJ Ellipse for close to nine years. The move from New York had been smooth only because the firm agreed to let her work from the D.C. office. But Gina wasn't too happy with her new team member. She wanted to get her own girl in the door. Last year, Gina gave her a rating of 3 (meets expectations) in her performance appraisal, which in Eira's opinion was fair considering she had been distracted with the move while closing the Shikhar chapter forever. But this year it was different. She'd given her 200% and the client satisfaction reviews, and multiple industry awards were there to prove it. And even though she wasn't Gina's favourite disciple, Eira knew she'd outperformed the rest. Technically, there was nothing that could stop her moving to the next grade. It was only a matter of a few weeks, and the appraisal rounds would begin again. With the bump in salary, Eira could finally make the down payment on her very first home. She'd waited long enough for it; first, it was paying off her student loans, then the larger home rentals with Zasha growing up and needing her own room, and everything else in between. Her moment of stability and permanency was finally here. No more renting. She was going to soon be a homeowner and put down roots.

'Gina seems happy with you.' Alice chirped, placing the white ink correction pen back into Eira's stationary holder.

'Is that her happy face?' Eira grinned, pulling a new retail client's half-finished floor plan from her drawer.

'She was praising you this morning and telling the interns they should aspire to be like you, well not those exact words but close. I'm guessing you're up for a promotion and going to be my boss soon.' Alice winked. She was a top performer too, but she didn't mind Eira as her direct supervisor. They were friends; Alice had tried playing matchmaker too. First, it was Joe from finance, a widower with no children, and an inherited sea-facing holiday home at Martha's Vineyard. Then came Noah from engineering who was a perfect match in Alice's book of soulmates. He was a divorcée with a son a year younger than Zasha, who visited on alternate weekends. But Noah wasn't interested in getting hitched again. *Never gonna take a bite of that tasteless apple again,* he joked during happy hours. And finally, there was Bryan. He was single and came with no baggage. The only problem with this pairing: he was the Vice President of the firm. Bryan had his eye on Eira right from her New York days. In fact, he'd made the inter-city transition possible by tossing Gina's recommendation out the window in seconds. After eight lunches of much discussion and cajoling, Eira finally gave into Alice's fantasy and went out for drinks with Bryan. But Eira wasn't ready to date just yet. The scar hadn't healed. Shikhar had lied and cheated her of the dreams he made her believe in. She'd loved a man who was now serving a prison sentence. Eira found it hard to trust any other human being at face value. Besides, if it didn't work out with Bryan, she'd be looking for a new job. A dating adventure was a luxury single mothers couldn't indulge in, and so even though she did like him she made their first date so unbearable – Zasha and her mother being the main topic of discussion – that he didn't ask her out a second time. Eira was relieved to have dodged a bullet.

'So, how's your doctor doing?' Alice got into her do-tell position, pressing her chin forward and crossing her arms across her chest. 'Treating you right?'

'Not now, I have to get this done by EOD or Gina's going to have my head on a platter. I was supposed to submit this two days ago.' Eira wriggled out of a potentially long dissection of her love life. Besides, Nikki was now her official therapist.

'Cool. We can talk at lunch.' Alice slumped her shoulders, not too pleased with Eira's response. If it hadn't been for her, Nihal and Eira may have never become a couple. Alice was fully invested in Eira's relationship; it was her mission to get Eira off the singles bus once and for all.

It was quarter past two and Nihal still hadn't called. Except for weekends, they spoke every noon after lunch, unless he was scheduled or pulled in for a surgery. He would text her if that were the case. But today, there were no text messages. Was he still mad at her? But there was no real reason to be pissed off. She had just refused to spend the night at his place, she reasoned. Eira hoped he would sleep off their last conversation and not talk about it. She just had to be patient.

'Cake?' Alice slid a plate with two slices of coffee cake towards Eira. 'Joe's fiancé baked it.'

'Joe, has a fiancé?'

'Yea.' Alice blinked twice, her eyebrows bunching at the centre of her forehead. 'I told you he was a catch.'

'Whatever.' Eira ignored Alice's comment and turned towards the TV screen mounted on the wall in the cafeteria.

BREAKING NEWS: *CEO Samuel Smith of KIC Pharmaceuticals sentenced to nine years in prison for insider trading and 4.2 million dollars in fines,* the red ticker running across the lower bottom of the screen read. The news anchor, Katy Jerry was giving live updates from outside the courtroom. Alice went red in the face. Her eyes darted to Eira and then fixed on the TV screen again.

'Excuse me.' Eira scraped back her chair. 'I just remembered I had to call my client.' She ad-libbed.

Eira walked back to her office and shut the door. The pain and sadness of losing Shikhar had been pushed to the backrooms of her brain, but the shame of being the girlfriend of the mastermind behind a major financial fraud still haunted her. When she met Shikhar Sen, he was a portfolio manager at Walker Asset Management. He rose to stardom with Momentum trades making millions for his clients. He was the boy with the magic touch on Wall Street. One wiretapping was all it took to bring him down to his knees and with him they were all dragged into the boiling pot. He became the poster boy for all insider trading catastrophes two years running. The media had their cameras following Eira, and her photos were plastered all over the news channels and across the front pages of the leading newspapers. Top anchors at every media house covered the scandal relentlessly, and experts were brought in for their opinion on the great Indian origin fund manager's rise and fall. Eira was taken in for questioning, and her personal accounts monitored. After a three-month investigation, she was finally given a clean bill of health.

'Did you or did you not tip off the CEO of Brown Financial Holdings about Plan Computers falling stock?' Eira roared, the vein in her forehead twisting rapidly.

'It's not that simple, and I can't explain.' Shikhar's voice was dull and listless. It had lost its usual confidence.

'You're out on bail. They haven't cleared your name, Shikhar. I need to know if you're innocent. Are they on a witch hunt or did you do it? I don't have time for any more lies or manipulation. I have a child who's become the butt of jokes in school, and I still get ridiculous calls from reporters at my workplace.' Her heart twisted with revolting anger, the resentment thickening in her throat.

'You need to get yourself a lawyer Eira. There are many heavyweights involved in this scam. I can't tell you more. If I do, you become party to the mess, and I don't want to drag you into it.' He folded his right fist into a ball and wiped the beads of sweat that had formed on his upper lip.

'And you suddenly grew a conscience?' Eira's voice was a decibel higher. 'After all this, now you realize that I'm getting screwed for no fault of mine? I hate you. I hate you so much I could poke you in the eye right now. I have never felt this ashamed in my life, not even when I got to know I was pregnant in college. I curse the day I met you, Shikhar. I hope you rot in hell.' She hissed. 'Goodbye.'

Eira walked out of his house and slammed the door behind her, willing her tears not to fall in front of him. Shikhar didn't follow her or try to stop her. He knew it was the end. He had ruined his life and theirs too. He loved Eira, but he'd let his greed guide his ambition too far.

One hour more and I can leave for the day, Eira told herself, hitting the keys on her laptop with calculated swiftness. She'd spent the last half hour in the restroom going over every scene in the courtroom the day Shikhar was convicted. Eira eschewed watching the national news or even listening to the radio. Watching someone else get convicted and their families ripped apart publicly, opened the floodgates to the nightmarish memories she had lived through.

Eira was now on her second last email when her desk phone rang.

'Hello, this is Eira,' she answered.

'Hey.'

'Hi.' Eira was relieved to hear Nihal's voice. It was now a quarter past four; a late call, but a call nonetheless.

'Are you avoiding me?'

'No. Why? Your phone's switched off. I tried calling you a few times and then had to claw through my drawer to find the only visiting card I had for you.'

'Sorry. The battery must have drained.' Eira apologized, digging in her bag for the phone charger.

'Do you have plans after work? I'd like to see you for a bit.'

'No plans. It's been a long day, and I'm dead beat. Can you meet me at Harry's Grill? It's two blocks from my house. We can grab a quick dinner, and I can get home at a decent time too.'

'Sure, see you in an hour.' Nihal clicked the phone shut.

It's a Thursday night. Nihal meets the boys for a beer on Thursdays. He never bails on them. What does he want to talk about? Does he want to take time off from us? Is he breaking off with me? Eira's mind raced at Bolt speed. *Oh, if only I could just erase last night. Why did I have to act on impulse! Impulsiveness is carelessness, silly cow,* she reprimanded herself all the way to Harry's Grill.

Chapter Five

'Table for two.' Eira requested. She'd reached a few minutes early and decided to seat herself before Nihal arrived. It gave her time to compose herself. Thinking for two people in a relationship was tiring. *What he thought. What she said. What he meant.* "Dating is a waste of precious time." Gina would often say when their colleagues ditched the singles train. But again, Gina had been with one man since college, and they were a boring, happily married couple.

'Hey.' Nihal leaned in and planted a soft kiss on her ear lobe. He was right on time. Nihal ordered his regular grilled steak with garlic butter and mashed potato, while she studied the menu for a couple of minutes more, finally going with baked salmon and a side.

'About last night.' Eira cleared her throat. 'It came out all wrong. We got all fired up and then you...' Eira bit her lower lip, '...it was embarrassing.'

'Eira, I'm turning forty next year. I'm serious about you; this is not a fling for me. I love that you came to see me the way you did last night. I've been thinking about you all morning.'

'All morning?'

'Yes. I waited until you wrapped up work at the office. I know you have your hands full with that new client's presentation and at home with a teenage daughter. It can't be easy. But I need to know if you're serious about us. It's been five months since we've been seeing each other. I haven't even been to your house; we only drive by it. I'm not mad at you, but this schedule thing is just silly. I want us to spend a weekend together, meet each other's friends and family. The guys think I have an imaginary girlfriend.'

'I hear you Nihal, and I want the same. I'm going to try and work something out.' Eira unwrapped the fork and knife from the paper napkin and arranged them on either side of her plate.

'Why won't you tell your family about me? Are you not sure about us?'

'I—'

'I love you Eira. I want us to be a real couple.'

And he said it.

'This is not the way I had planned to tell you how I feel, but with our schedules and your family hide-and-seek, it's impossible to plan a candlelight dinner with you.' He fidgeted with the butter knife. 'Are you even looking at us as a long-term relationship? I need to know because I'm certain that's what I want with you.'

'I really like you. I may even love you, but it's complicated, and that's what I was getting to before you told me you love me.'

'Like me? Are you asking for time to think?'

'No. I didn't say that.'

'Then what are you saying?' Nihal demanded.

'I'm trying here.'

'Sorry. Go ahead.'

'Zasha found out about us, and we had a blowout yesterday, and then this morning I told my mother about you because I need her help in winning back my daughter's trust.'

'So Zasha is not fond of me right now, but that's because she doesn't know me. I don't expect us to be backslapping buddies at the first go.'

'No Nihal. She kinda hates you right now. She will hate any man who tries to enter our family.' Eira's eyelids lowered. 'Our family has been through a lot, and that's the reason I didn't tell anyone about us, not even my best friend. I wanted to be a hundred percent sure. This is all new to me. I've been in control for so long, and now I'm doing stupid things like driving to see you late at night and making out in a parking lot. Surely that has to mean something.' Eira tilted her head to the side. 'There's no logical explanation for that. The truth is… I'm crazy about you, Nihal. I love you too.' Eira rested her fingers gently over his warm hands. 'It feels good saying it out loud.'

A broad smile spread across Nihal's face. 'You are so beautiful, Eira.' He stroked her supple skin from the edge of her lips to her cheek bone. 'I wish we weren't in a restaurant right now, or I'd take you in my arms and devour that gorgeous mouth.'

'I would have liked that too.' They drifted into a silent glimmer of a hopeful future.

'Well,' Nihal took a deep breath. 'What does your mother think about us? Does she hate me too?'

'She didn't say too much. We were in the car when I told her.'

'You sprang this on her in your car?' The lines around his mouth deepened. 'You really are something else.'

'I told you, you're making me do crazy things. I don't talk to my mother about my love life, and yet, here I am doing exactly that.'

Nihal clasped her hands and stroked her thumb reassuringly. His eyes were smiling down at hers. *Is this the lovesick puppy look Zasha was talking about?* Eira's heart was now doing the Macarena. A cloud of doubt had lifted. She could now confidently answer her mother's *Do you love him* question. Sometimes you just have to say it out aloud to know if you do, and they'd both said it to each other. It was right.

It fitted well. The timing was perfect too. She could now bring up the meet-my-folks conversation.

'There's something else.' Eira retracted her hand from his as the waiter set their orders down on the table. 'My mother wants to meet you.'

'Awesome. Let's do it right after we eat. I'm ready.' Nihal cracked a smile.

'Nihal.'

'Right. I forgot. We got to check the schedules.' He took a jab at his meat.

'She's expecting you for a proper chat, and my daughter will be there too. So, let's do this right.' Eira flipped through her phone calendar and double tapped her screen. 'How about on the Saturday of Memorial Day weekend? We're all home, and you have the day off too. Does that work?'

'I can do ten more days of being the mystery lover. Besides, it gives me time to practice my introduction and floor the Deys with my fabulous sense of humour.'

'Okay, so here's the thing. Can you just be your normal self? They'll be eyeing you like hawks, so if you slip up, they'll swoop down on you with their claws in your flesh.' Eira's eyes were now wide and animated. 'And please don't do your impressions. I love them, and they are funny, but save them for a later time, when they're ready for it.'

'Are you trying to scare me off? I thought of doing my Bugs Bunny act.'

'She's twelve, not four!'

'Homer Simpson…Bart maybe?' Nihal persisted.

'No. No impressions. Don't do funny. Just be yourself minus the funny.' Eira pleaded.

'Alright. You have an extensive list of don'ts.' Nihal nodded his head in defeat forking up a piece of lettuce from her plate.

'I know my family, and I want this to go well,' Eira wrinkled her nose and twisted her mouth, 'so please stick with my list.' She begged.

'And what if I don't like them and find *them* annoying?'

'They can be annoying, but they're my family. So tough luck. Suck it up and don't tell me.'

'Are you going to instruct them to be on their best behaviour too?' Nihal arched an eyebrow with a puckish grin slapped on his lips.

'Oh ha, bloody ha. Come on eat up. It's getting late, and I must get going. Heavy-duty meeting with my mother tonight.' They finished the rest of their meal in blissful silence pleased with the way the evening had progressed. From a secret relationship just two days ago, they'd dived into commitment and had even fixed a date to meet her family.

When Eira got home later that evening, Zasha was in a perky mood. She'd scored two As and an A+ at school. Earphones plugged in, she whistled the bars of a popular song while helping her grandmother lay the table. Eira was going to have to eat two dinners that night. Kanika would throw a fit if she knew Eira had eaten out a third time that week: Monday was dinner with clients; Tuesday was Gina's birthday bash, and today was a must-have. But she was going to spare them the details of her previous dinner.

'Eira, I've tried a new chicken curry recipe today. Tell me what you think?' Kanika asked, scooping some steamed rice on to her plate.

Eira watched Zasha serve herself a generous portion of the previous night's leftover *bhindi* that she'd made and pour a drizzle of the chicken curry over her rice. Zasha knew she was being watched and controlled her smile, but her eyes crinkled. Kanika made an honest effort at trying out different cuisines, but the truth was hard to hide – she was a pathetic cook. Her spice levels were never right. It was either too hot or too mild. But idlis, those steamed rice pillows, they were made to perfection every time. Eira, on the other hand, was a Master Chef with the knives. She loved experimenting with new ingredients and seasonal foods. Eira didn't entertain regularly, but when she did no one missed an Eira Dey party.

'It's good Mummy. I like the tamarind flavour in the curry.' Eira complimented Kanika's effort and took another spoonful of rice.

'Have some more.' Kanika offered enthusiastically, but Eira was sated from her previous meal.

'I'll take some to work with me tomorrow,' Eira dodged.

'If you don't like it just say it, don't patronize me.' Kanika slumped in her chair. 'Zasha has barely touched the curry.'

'No Mummy. Honestly, it is good.'

'Nani, the gravy is good. I didn't take the chicken because I've been toying with the idea of turning vegetarian.'

'Did Nani's chicken curry make you convert to vegetarianism?' Eira tittered.

'Not funny at all.' Kanika shot at Eira's infantile sense of humour.

'I want to reduce my carbon footprint. I'm doing my bit.'

'Are you nuts?' Eira spat out an uncrushed pepper from her mouth. 'Is this one of your many experiments?'

'I'm serious, Mom.'

'Cool, so I don't need to buy anymore boneless chicken to suit your no-meat-on-bone requirement.' Eira turned towards her mother for a nod of allegiance, but Kanika was in no mood for a high five. 'Okay, I did something today, and I want to explain why I did what I did. So, no jumping in before I finish.' Eira instructed. 'No eye-rolling either.'

'Zasha, that last part was for you.' Kanika said, taking a second helping of the salad.

'Whatever.' Zasha muttered under her breath. She opened her mouth as if to say more, then rolled her tongue to the inside of her cheek and looked down at her plate. She knew what was coming next: her mother was going to tell them she'd broken up with Dr Zane and blame her for her loveless life. But this was a good decision. It would all work out for the best. They didn't need a man in their family. They were doing just fine all these years until Shikhar walked into their lives, but they were strong women and had pulled it together. She didn't need a father figure. She was happy to spend time with her biological father during his visits.

'Sheesh, this isn't easy.' Eira let out a nervous laugh and fell back in her chair. This was turning out to be harder than she had anticipated. She leaned forward once again and loosely knotted her fingers on the table. 'Well, now that both of you know about me seeing a certain gentleman for the past few months, I want you'll to have the complete story.'

'But why?' Zasha interrupted. 'If you broke up with him, we don't need to know anymore.'

'I said wait until I finish what I have to say.' Eira kept her eyes fixed on her entwined fingers and exhaled deeply. 'Mummy, I don't know if you remember, but Dr Nihal Zane was Zasha's operating paediatrician when she fractured her wrist the month we moved to D.C.'

Kanika drew a blank. She tried to jog her memory, but she just couldn't put a face to the name.

'Never mind. That's how I first met him and then we met again six months ago at Alice's bachelorette party. He happened to be at the same pub we were at, and we got talking. A few days later, I got a call from him. He'd looked me up the hospital patient directory. I had dropped my gym membership card at the pub, and he wanted to return it to me. Nihal offered to send it in the mail, but I insisted on picking it up. I didn't want to put him through any trouble. It was just a membership card. We had coffee together at the hospital cafeteria, and we talked for about an hour. It was like we'd been friends for a long time and not as if we had just met a night before. I didn't think we'd get involved in a serious relationship. I just liked having someone to talk to…it was refreshing to meet someone new.'

'Mom, where does this grand introduction lead?'

'Zasha, your mother is talking. I think we can give her ten minutes without interrupting.' Kanika jerked her head. She sensed that her daughter wasn't about to tell them she'd broken up with Nihal, this was something else. Eira sounded as if she had it under control, but would Zasha be able to handle it?

'We're in love.' Eira's voice was surprising in its intensity and conviction. 'We're not breaking up, and I want you to meet him first, Zasha, before you run him down. He's a lovely man.'

'I don't mean to rain on your parade, but don't they all start out "lovely" and then land up in prison?' Zasha barked.

'Shikhar was a mistake. A Goliath-size mistake. But there were no signs, I could not have imagined he would turn out to be a fraud. I know you got hurt. I did too. I am sorry you had to go through all of that. I am your mother; I feel your pain.'

'Do you? First Dad was a mistake, then Shikhar. But I'm saving you from making another mistake, Mom. Dr Zane is a ticking bomb.' Zasha concluded in her debate-team tone.

'Sweetheart.' Eira tried to keep her voice calm. 'You don't know him. Your animosity towards him is a reaction to what you've been through, and I understand your fear, but we can't live under a shell. Sometimes the risk is worth taking.'

'Mom this is not about just protecting you from another disaster.' Zasha's arms were now in the air. 'I don't want to dream about having the perfect family because we can't. Just look at us.' Zasha protested, her volume rising.

'Eira, what is it that you did today?' Kanika interjected, giving her daughter a window to say what was on her mind. She was surprised by Eira's declaration of love considering just that morning she'd spoken about not being in a neatly defined relationship. Maybe she had figured it out during the course of the day or maybe she always was in a defined relationship and wasn't ready to talk about them yet.

'I've invited him over for dinner on Memorial Day weekend, and I would like you'll to meet him. He is looking forward to this dinner.' Eira dipped her head, and her eyes strayed toward Zasha waiting for an answer.

'Sounds lovely. I'm in,' Kanika stepped up.

'Fine. I don't have an option. I have to sit through this dinner, so I'll be there. Any rules that need to be followed?' Zasha grimaced.

'Thank you for doing this,' Eira said. There were no rules. Any specific instructions would have the exact opposite of the desired outcome.

'Can Mia join us for dinner?' Zasha gave it a long shot.

'Dr Zane isn't a zoo exhibit. Mia is a wonderful girl and a great friend to you, but this is a family dinner,' Kanika explained.

Eira grazed a thank you glance at her mother. Nihal had to see her family for who they were; if this was Zasha going through a phase he had to experience first-hand what it would be like living with a teen child.

Chapter Six

Zasha retreated to her room early that night. The lights in her room were out by 9.30 p.m. This behaviour was unlike her. If something was bothering her, she would be on the phone bearing her heart out to Mia making Eira *sshh* her to keep their animated, loud conversations confined to her room. But despite Eira's mega announcement, there was no phone call that night. Eira knocked a light tap on Zasha's door; there was no response. So, she cracked the door open and peeped in—Zasha still followed the rules, no locks on doors—to find Zasha asleep, letting out soft snores just like she did when she was a baby in her panda print onesie.

Eira's pregnancy hadn't been an easy one with Zasha all geared up to make her debut on earth at seven months. However, Eira was determined to stick to the schedule. She was going to birth a full-term baby and make it to the 38-week finishing line, and so she took a cervical stitch. In her eight month, the kicking was hellish. Eira felt as if she was growing a mini-David Beckham inside her womb, who was hitting hard at the walls of her uterus. But when a nine-pound Zasha finally popped out after a twelve-hour long labour, she was the most easy going and supportive baby. She was perfect with a tuft of soft brown hair on her round head and a cleft in her chin like Dhruv, her biological father. Barring her brown eyes, Zasha was a spitting image of Dhruv. She had his light Punjabi skin tone and lean frame. Their lips pouted in the same way when they were angry. It was both endearing and annoying to see her resemble him to such a large extent. Eira had read and heard of the dreaded witching hour that exhausted first-time parents couldn't escape. But Zasha wasn't a colicky or demanding baby; she began sleeping through the night at six months. Much to Eira's surprise, Zasha took to the bottle minus any drama and gulped down several ounces of pumped milk without a fuss each day. At six, she was lecturing her mother about the importance of eating veggies for lunch and dinner. A straight-A student, Zasha was a sociable child and never got into any trouble at school. But that was until they moved cities. While her grades didn't drop, Zasha was no longer the fun-loving, easy going child she used to be in New York. She'd swapped her rainbow-coloured cape for a dark and grim one, picking and slicing everything her mother did or said. With the kicking and aggressive behaviour resurfacing, Eira felt as if she was pregnant all over again.

Eira kissed Zasha goodnight and left the room. She stepped out of her puffy slippers and onto the hardwood floor of her bedroom. It was cold, and the floorboards creaked. She climbed into bed and rested her back against the mahogany headboard. The house was quiet. In the moonlight, the new leaves on the red maple tree standing right in front of their house shone like silver buntings. She could hear the sea shell wind chimes hanging from Kanika's bedroom window, dancing in the spring breeze. The fragrance of spring flowers wafted through her bedroom. Kanika had a green thumb and had set up a tiny yet pretty bed of roses, daffodils, and tulips in their front lawn. Eira slipped under the covers and waited patiently to fall asleep, but sleep had escaped her eyes. She got up and sat upright in bed. Her eyes fell on a frame that carried a picture of her with Baby Zasha in her arms. That picture of the two of them stared blankly at her. All those years gone by, her first tooth, those first steps, the laughter and gurgles, the sleepless nights trying to balance motherhood and a career. *A journey I chose and one that I'm supremely proud of,* she reminded herself. Eira closed her eyes, and there he was, Dhruv Kapur, skipping around in her mind. Memories of Dhruv deluged her mind, and she let herself remember those two weeks that changed her life forever.

15 March 2004

Cornell University, New York, USA

'I'm so glad you are coming along and not being a nerd spending spring break with Kanika aunty. This trip to Miami is going to be wicked,' Nikki chirped. 'Did I mention my brother will be joining us too? You've met him, right?'

'No. I've only seen your brother's geeky teenage photos that you've stuck on your soft board.'

'Oh right. You didn't join us for Thanksgiving. You keep missing out on all the fun.'

'Perks of living with a single-earning-parent.' Eira deadpanned.

'Don't make me feel guilty about spending my father's money. It's okay. They have enough,' Nikki consoled herself.

'Ha ha you did feel a little guilty, didn't you?'

'Just for a second. Thanks to you.'

'I'm able to come along for spring break this year, only because I opted out of a visit to India to see my dad. For three years now, since Mummy and I moved to New York, we've been the ones visiting him during the holidays. That makes two tickets. I don't see him getting on a twenty-two-hour flight, and I'm okay with that. Strangely, Mummy agreed. She didn't need much convincing. Although, she was concerned about your boyfriend, Sai, tagging along. Only when I mentioned you'd invited your female roommates too, she relaxed. But now I'm going to have to tell her about your brother too. I'll keep that minute detail for after we're back from Miami.' Eira had to be cautious. She didn't want to muddle up this trip. 'What's the deal with your bro?'

'Dhruv's slogging his ass in Boston. He's plankton at McKinsey, at least that's what he says. But he has his ten-year plan chalked out, and he's dedicated, so I'm pretty sure he'll get there. Dhruv's the smarter one between the two of us you know, and the more sensible one too, in other words, "boring."' Nikki drew finger quotes in the air. 'To be honest, I'm glad he's the smarter one, thanks to his success story, I got to study in the US too. I kept using the *Dhruv hai na, Papa* spiel and my folks finally agreed to let their only daughter travel *saat samundar par* to study.'

'You're a con artist. You really bully your parents.' Eira giggled. 'Come to think of it, in the three years that I've known you, Dhruv has never visited you on campus.'

'We meet each other in December in Mumbai when we're back home,' Nikki snickered. 'My parents need an *in case of an emergency* plan. It didn't matter that he lived on the west coast when I applied for University. They were simply happy that we were both in the same country. I didn't argue with that logic.' Nikki continued throwing clothes into her duffle bag. 'Dhruv's the boring kind, nothing exciting ever happens in his life. And just FYI, he's not into girls.'

'He's gay?' Eira's eyes widened.

'Ha ha. No.' Nikki spluttered, throwing herself dramatically on the clothes lying on her bed. 'Mummy would kill you if she heard that. Her son is a catch. Dhruv's just too focused. If I remember correctly, the last time he was dating someone was two years ago, but she dumped him. I guess Dhruv spent more time talking to her about his ten-year plan than showing her a good time.' Nikki giggled.

'So why is Mr Boring joining us for spring break?' Eira pressed a travel size bottle of shampoo in a Ziploc, sliding her fingers across the interlocking ridges to seal the bag.

'I invited him. He sounded pretty beat on the phone. He hasn't been on a vacation in two years. It's pretty cut-throat at McKinsey.' Nikki's voice had a certain sense of pride, but she was also solicitous about his well-being. 'Besides, he's the one who got us this super deal with a beachfront view. It's his colleague's holiday home.'

'Hmm. Our 20s are for burning the midnight oil. Fifteen years down, he'll be thanking himself that he did.' Eira remarked as if repeating out of a self-help book, in her case this book would be Kanika's philosophy of life.

'Honey, we're officially *off* coursework for a week.' Nikki placed her finger on Eira's lips to quieten her. 'No more goals and life plans. It's beer, sun and sand for this week. Come on, let's go, our taxi is here.'

'Miami, here we come!' Eira fist pumped the air with delight to show spring break solidarity.

This was Eira's first visit to Florida, and she was particularly excited about getting away from New York's bone-biting five-month-long winter. Eira skimmed through the brochure display at the airport and picked up a bunch of city maps, food guides and *Things to see in Miami* brochures. Her backpack was filled with printouts of all the free activities that they could do in Miami, but Nikki was more interested in wearing a new bikini every day and lying on the beach with a chilled beer. The girls cut a deal – one touristy activity for three inactive hours at the beach.

'This is gorgeous.' Eira tipped her head back looking up at the newly remodelled beach rental they would call home for the next seven days. The bungalow's lemon-yellow walls beamed in the afternoon sun. Eira took a moment to appreciate the sundown orange bougainvillea that climbed up the trellised, street-facing wall.

'Dhruv's here already,' Nikki guessed. 'I can hear Pink Floyd playing.'

'This place is huge,' Sai yelped, dragging two bags across the gravel driveway.

'I'm out here, come see the view.' Dhruv's voice echoed through the house.

'So, *this* is what you're working so hard for.' Nikki inhaled the saltiness of the air and soaked in the ocean view.

'This is my colleague's ancestral home. He's at the bottom of the corporate pyramid too, just like me. Yea, but I do hope someday I can have all this,' Dhruv said, popping a chilled Heineken open. 'Where's the rest of your crew?'

'Sai's giving them a tour of the house.'

'Explorers,' Dhruv chortled, embracing his sister in a giant bear hug. 'Good to see you, sis.'

Eira appeared from behind the glass sliding doors, the only solid structure separating her from the saline tang of the ocean. Dhruv spun around to face her, and her lips quirked in a soft smile.

'Hey, I'm Dhruv, Nikki's elder brother.' Dhruv held out his hand, his grip was warm and welcoming.

'This is my geeky brother I was talking about.' Nikki added, wrapping her arm around his neck.

'She calls everyone who's smarter than her geeky.' Dhruv punched his sister playfully in the arm. 'Do I look geeky to you?' He asked, knocking back his beer.

No, just unbearably gorgeous! Eira was trying not to say, but if he could read her mind, she would have to hide in the closet for the rest of the trip. Dhruv was a female version of his sister with luminous greyish green eyes and soft brown hair that ended just above his ears. His calves and forearms were taut with muscle like someone who played sport. *Tennis? Football?* Her mind wandered. Nikki was a good athlete too and went for a run every morning come snow or sunshine. They were the sporty siblings, she concluded.

'Wazzup!' Sai joined the trio on the deck. 'Nikki your roommates have made themselves comfortable in the far-left bedroom upstairs. It's the largest one in the house. And I've kept our bags in the one next to theirs.'

'You're sharing a room?' Dhruv asked with a puckish smile. Nikki and Sai exchanged a sceptical look. 'Gotcha!' Dhruv beamed. 'I love doing this to you, and you fall for it every time.' The boys burst out laughing.

'Sorry, Eira. You're going to have to wake up to a garden view.' Sai tried to be as earnest as possible.

'Well, I was the last to join the fun, so that's cool.'

'You can take my room if you like. It's half-and-half, best of both views,' Dhruv cut in.

'Oooh. How gentlemanly of you!' Nikki prattled, slouching back in one of the five large beach chairs on the deck. 'Come, sit with me, Eira, before my brother starts hitting on you.'

'I'm being a good host, lil sis.' Dhruv ruffled Nikki's hair, trying to hide his embarrassment.

'Thanks, Dhruv. I'm okay with the room.'

'Alright then, let's get this party started.' Sai pawed through the ice box and drew out two bottles of cranberry Smirnoff for Nikki's roommates, who'd finally joined them on the deck.

Later that evening the girls got busy trying on their Friday night best. Clothes were scattered on the floor in all three bathrooms. The two boys were banished down to the tiny bathroom on the ground floor.

'Everyone's above twenty-one here, right?' Dhruv enquired.

'Yes,' they chorused, amused by him going all *big daddy* on them.

'Ms Dey is our newest entrant,' Nikki added. Just what Eira needed, to be called the baby of the group. Eira shrugged off her best friend's earlier observation about Dhruv hitting on her, as if it were a figment of her feral imagination. If only she knew, from the moment she got down those stairs wearing a fitting, olive green halter dress that ended three inches above her knees, Dhruv's eyes had been following her around. Eira was curvaceous in all the right places, and she knew to pick cuts and prints that flattered her body.

'Our ride's here,' Dhruv called out, pointing to a white limousine parked on the palm-tree-lined street. 'That's on me, sis.'

'I wasn't going to split the money. I'm good with the *kaali peeli* cabs of Miami.' Nikki sidled over and whispered in Eira's ears, 'He's being clumsy, but that's him flirting with you.'

'I don't think so. I'm his little sister's friend, that's all. He's probably into wine glass clinking women dressed in fashionable business suits. He's what…seven years older than us?'

'Nope, five years. So, you have the hots for him too?' Nikki teased. 'Or you wouldn't be worrying about the *"type"* of women he went for.'

'Oh stop,' Eira fumbled. 'I was only stating the obvious, and I am not interested in being in a relationship. It's too much work.'

'Okay, so just have fun. Fine by me.' Nikki cackled, easing into a light-weight leather jacket. 'I'm sure he wouldn't mind either.'

'Shh keep your voice down. Stop being stupid.' Eira hooked Nikki's elbow and dragged her out the front door before Sai joined in the ragging.

Chapter Seven

Club Havana resembled an old industrial warehouse from the outside. With five bars, three dance floors and different music playing in each, Club Havana was *"the place"* to be during spring break. Eira wasn't much of a dancer, but she was enjoying the vibe of the club. Nikki had taken off with Sai, and they were heating up the dance floor with their moves. The other two girls had met some of their friends from high school and were engrossed in catch-up conversations. Dhruv watched Eira from afar. Her head was bobbing to the beat of a hip-hop song he'd heard only for the first time. She was oblivious of the screaming club-goers grooving behind her on the dance floor. Dhruv was on his third pint now. Something in the air was making him gulp down his alcohol. The night was just getting started.

'Too loud?' Dhruv asked, bringing his mouth close to her ear. His warm breath made the skin of her neck prickle. Eira jumped an inch off her stool and sat down again when she realized it was Dhruv.

'Sorry, I didn't mean to scare you.' Dhruv apologized, trying to stay at a respectable distance from her in a club that had people's backsides touching each other.

'Nikki still on the dance floor?'

'Yes, I think so. Sai won't let her get off so easily. You don't like dancing, or you don't like the music?' Dhruv prodded.

'It's all good. I'm in a floaty place.' Eira gave him a benign smile and continued to suck on the olive on her toothpick. Her eyes were sparkling like cut glass, and she was smiling from ear to ear. They sipped on their drinks and flirted a little for the next half hour, and as the night wore on, all Dhruv wanted was to find a quieter place, where they could just sit and talk.

'Do you want to step out for some fresh air?' Dhruv could tell she was buzzed. Eira had swapped her favourite tipple—a beer for a Martini—attempting to be adventurous, but the second Martini had propelled her to a happy place she'd never visited before.

'Sounds good.' Clutching the bar counter Eira tried to steady herself to walk to the door.

'Are you drunk?' Dhruv was now worried.

'Pfft, just let it drop. I'm on my first spring break.' Eira snapped, her gold hoop earrings swinging as she looped the metal string of her purse around her shoulders.

'Sorry. I didn't mean to bug you. I just wanted to know if you could walk fine.'

Eira's face softened. Dhruv was being a gentleman and looking out for her, but she didn't want him to think she was a clichéd twenty-one-year-old, who couldn't choose her libation wisely. She placed her hand in his and held his gaze. No more talk. They walked out of the club together hand-in-hand.

Nestled on the southernmost tip of South Beach, Club Havana was a popular nightclub on that stretch. The space outside the club was as busy as the crowded nightclub they'd just left. They decided on a midnight paseo on the beach that was a stone's throw away. Dhruv held her strappy stilettos in one hand, while Eira held on to his other arm. Her feet were sinking in the cool night sand, and she was slowly floating away. Now that she was standing so close to him, Dhruv noticed how tiny she was without her heels.

The beach was silent with only the sound of small waves crashing against the shore. Their footprints followed them all the way to the water where the surf tickled their toes.

'Eira, I want to kiss you right now.' Dhruv said skittishly, his grey-green eyes dancing in a flood of moonlight. Behind his I-got-my-shit-together demeanour was hidden winsome boyish exuberance and oodles of charm.

'I want you to kiss me too.' Eira looked down at her feet, her bronze nails playing peek-a-boo with the sand. 'But only if you're not expecting this to get serious.'

'Understood. No strings attached.'

'No strings attached,' Eira repeated.

Dhruv leaned down bringing his face closer to her and lifted her chin. She tilted her head gently, and their lips brushed innocently. He planted a kiss on the tip of her nose, moving slowly down to her quivering lips he began to kiss her all over again. His moist lips parted, and he flicked her mouth open with the tip of his tongue. Dhruv went for a real kiss this time. Eira's hand eased across his chest slowly making its way to his lower back. He tasted the flavour of olives in her mouth. With a sudden sense of urgency, his arms tightened around her waist as he pressed his lips harder against hers.

'Wow,' she said, pulling back. 'This is crazy. It's getting chilly. We should go back inside.' Eira suggested, zipping up her jacket. The chemistry between them was raw. He was smitten by her, and he knew she thought his kissing was impressive too. Nestled under his arm, they walked back to the club smiling away to themselves.

Eira and Dhruv spent the next few days getting frisky in restrooms, stealing kisses every time someone left the room, cuddling in the backseat of a taxi (this took a great deal of seating manipulation to ensure they were the only two riding the taxi together). It was all risky fun, the thrill of carelessness that was driving them to explore uncharted territories. Just knowing that they'd probably never see each other again at least in a situation like this made them want each other even more, and then two nights before their week of adventure was over, they scrapped their no *sex-sex* deal and bit the forbidden fruit. *It was just sex!* Eira reminded herself the next morning as they said their goodbyes.

But three weeks later, when she didn't bleed into a sanitary napkin like she did every twenty-nine days, Eira panicked. She waited a few days more before she took a pregnancy test. They'd been careful and used protection. *Fucking condoms*, she yelled at the four pregnancy strips that lay open on her bathroom floor. *History was repeating itself* she thought, first she was an unplanned pregnancy and now this baby! At least her parents were married. Dhruv would never want to keep this baby, and why should he? They weren't a couple. Eira decided to take things into her own hand and made an appointment to get rid of it within the next couple of weeks. This had to be the best solution – they had their whole lives ahead of them – but her heart did a 180-degree flip when she saw the baby on the monitor. At first, it looked like fuzzy grey space, but then the doctor moved the scanner around on her abdomen, and the baby came into view. A small ark on the screen, approximately the size of a single lentil seed, and it all became real. She had a life growing inside of her. Eira had made one mistake getting pregnant, but she wasn't ready to make another by terminating the pregnancy. Eira decided to take responsibility for her actions, and so she chose to carry her unplanned pregnancy to term. But keeping the baby was probably an easier decision than convincing Dhruv that she didn't want to get married.

'Why do you want to keep this baby?' Dhruv snapped. 'To make me look stupid?'

'We're not a couple. We didn't plan this baby. Why do you want to get married? Do you love me?' Eira blustered. 'I don't.' She wrapped up before he could say *yes* which was a response she wasn't ready for, and a *no* would just be heart-pricking.

'We could. Hundreds of people in India do that every day. They get married and fall in love later. It's called an arranged marriage.' Dhruv made a feeble stab at humour. 'I like you, and we're physically compatible for sure. I have a decent job. We could make this work. But you have to give it a chance.'

'I don't see why we have to give this a chance. I am not in the right space to get into a committed relationship. I am not ready for motherhood either, but I know it is the right thing to do, and I want to do this. You and me, I don't see us building a life together.'

'What's wrong with me?' Dhruv was affronted by her refusal.

'Nothing. *Nothing* is wrong with you. But I don't want to get married. Stop forcing this relationship. If we're meant to be, we will, even if it takes us ten or twenty years. Right now, it's not happening.' Eira argued with little success at making her point.

'What about your mom?'

'What about her?' Eira thundered.

'Wouldn't she expect you to marry the father of your child?'

'She expected me not to get pregnant. I let her down.' *I've always been a disappointment to her* Eira thought. 'I am going to complete my course and do what I came to New York to do. This baby was never part of the plan, but I'm ready to bring it into this world. Marriage, I am certainly not ready for, and I'm not going to let you or her pressurize me into it. Marriage is a lot more than signing papers and sharing a bed,' Eira said with a petulant toss of her head.

'So, she does want you to get married.'

'Dhruv, you're not listening. I took my eyes off the ball once. I made one tiny mistake, and here I am today, pregnant. I'm not going to screw it up any further. So, here's what's going to happen. I'm going to petition for permission to take a gap year, and I'll stay with my mother through this pregnancy. I will resume my course next fall and will come home every weekend. Worst case scenario, if the University rejects my petition, I will continue with the course as is. It's going to be tough, but I'm up for the challenge. My mother has more or less agreed to pitch in and support me. So please don't go behind my back trying to get her to convince me to ditch my plan.'

'Eira, you don't have a clue about how stressful the last two years of your course will be, and you don't want to graduate last in your class. I can be there for you and the baby while you complete your education. What about the Master's program you talked about?'

'I've got this Dhruv.'

'No, you don't. You don't have jackshit. All you want to do is keep me as far away as possible from a child that is biologically mine, even though I'm happy to be part of his or her life.'

'No, you can visit my…our child whenever you want. Please believe me. We don't have to make this messy by involving the court to decide custody or visitation rights. We can amicably figure out the logistics later.'

At that moment, Dhruv realized he was pushing a woman who had already made up her mind, even before he had walked through her door. She never intended for a discussion. She was letting him know how things were going to pan out, and given the delicate situation she was in, he didn't want to stress her any further.

'I want to be there at every ultrasound, doctor's appointment, and when you go into labour too. I won't have it any other way,' Dhruv said firmly.

'Okay. Anything else?'

'And we get to decide the name of this child together.'

'Done.' Eira had no intention of depriving him of his rights, but she knew she had to look out for her own interest too. 'We can decide the baby's last name and how we share the holidays later. Cool?' She added.

'Sure. But my offer still stands, if you do change your mind.' Dhruv was persistent. He was determined to do what was best for their child just like his parents, who always put Nikki and him above their own needs and interests.

'I'll keep that in mind.'

For the next few months, until Zasha was born, Dhruv didn't bring up marriage. He hoped she would see sense in his proposal once they welcomed the baby into the world. Dhruv's heart swelled with pride the moment Zasha was placed in his arms an hour after she was born. He could see traces of himself in her already. But his joy was incomplete. He wanted them to be a family. He wanted to be there for his daughter and to be part of every milestone. Dhruv's parents were enraged by this arrangement. They were furious with their son for getting a woman pregnant, but they were angrier with Eira for rejecting his proposal.

'I'm moving back to the west coast, Eira. I've got a terrific job offer in San Francisco, and I'm taking it.' Dhruv announced on an orange-leafed Saturday morning, when he came to take three-year-old Zasha for the weekend.

'Oh, that's fantastic news.' Eira dissembled her true feelings from him. His physical presence in their life made her feel more confident about her parenting skills. He was her safety net, but she knew there would be a time when he would move on to newer things, work and even people. Those were the unsaid rules of their arrangement.

'I'm cashing in my chips. I've waited long enough hoping you'd change your mind. I did everything a good father does, but you won't give us a chance. Eira, I want to move forward, and I believe moving away will allow me to do so.'

'You are a good father, and Zasha is lucky to have you in her life,' Eira said. She enjoyed having Dhruv over and watching him spend time with their daughter, but the chemistry that existed the night she got pregnant had vanished forever. She could never look at him the same way again no matter how much she tried. He reminded her of the biggest mistake of her life.

'I'll visit as often as I can, and when Zasha's ready to be away from you for more than two nights I'd like to have her with me for longer.'

'Sounds good. All the best, Dhruv.' Eira came forward to give him a hug and lingered in his arms one last time. 'Thank you for always being there for us through these years. We will miss you.'

Not once did Eira doubt his commitment to their daughter, and just as she had expected, despite the geographical distance Dhruv was always available for Zasha. His little girl only had to say the word, and he would get on a flight that very weekend.

Buzz. Buzz. Eira's phone vibrated jerking her out of her reverie. It was a message from Nihal.

Missing you. Thinking about your surprise visit last night ☺

She checked her bedside clock – 11 p.m. it glowed in the dark – Nihal was on his way home.

Me too, she typed back and set her phone to rest.

Focus on the Memorial Day dinner, Eira, she reminded herself. *Don't get sucked into the past.*

Chapter Eight

24 May 2017

New York, USA

'I'll miss you, but I'm glad you're going to Mumbai and spending time with your family,' Sai said, kissing the tip of Nikki's nose.

'Thank you for being my rock, Sai.'

'I love you. You don't need to thank me for anything. Sweetheart, I have a gut feeling, and it's a positive one. The surrogacy agency will come back with good news,' Sai crossed his fingers.

Life hadn't turned out the way Nikki had expected. It had thrown her a curveball. After five years of trying every trick in the book: flat on her back, legs in the air, she still wasn't pregnant. All the pencilled-in lovemaking had worn her out physically, mentally, and emotionally. Sex had become more mechanical, like one of the many things on her monthly to-do list. After their scheduled sexual gymnastics, she would religiously get into the *Viparita Karani* position – bottom hoisted in the air. Sai would hold her legs up for additional support, so it wouldn't hurt her back. As popular folklore went, thousands of women were impregnated in this manner. So, she would lie in bed in the uncomfortable position, while fervently hoping not to get her period for the next nine months.

The last seven months were the worst; they had spent hundreds of dollars on IVF treatments. A day before the egg retrieval procedure, going against his agnostic beliefs, Sai would secretly visit the ISKCON temple on Long Island and plead, beg, bribe, and cut deals with God. No matter how many eggs Nikki released, not even one fertilised.

Her parents tiptoed around the adoption conversation. Sai was more than willing, but Nikki kept stalling. Despite multiple failed attempts, she was unwilling to accept that they may never be able to have a biological child of their own. Nikki was closed to the idea of donor eggs and wanted her own baby – her flesh and blood. But then, a few months ago, her father-in-law who'd seen her drowning in a burning desire for her own child decided to give them some parental advice.

'*Beta*, I don't mean to interfere in your personal affairs, but there is something I want to share with you'll. Please hear me out completely before dismissing the idea,' Sai's dad said cautiously.

'Sure, dad,' Nikki willingly agreed.

'Have you considered a surrogate?' He proceeded.

The air in the room grew tense. There was a long silence, punctuated only by the ticking of the wall clock.

'No, we haven't,' Sai replied.

'Maybe, you should give it some thought.' Sai's father had said the unthinkable.

How DARE he? Nikki looked down into her bowl of soup and felt tears welling up in her eyes. The sadness soon turned to anger, and she bit her lower lip as hard as she could to stop her thoughts from escaping her mouth. *He wants me to get a womb on lease!* The mere thought of another woman bearing her child made her anxious. But she was slowly running out of options, and she knew it. Sai didn't want her to make any decisions in a hurry. In fact, after that meal, he never spoke about surrogacy again. Nikki, of course, couldn't shake off that conversation and did her own research on assisted pregnancies. A month later, Sai, and she finally agreed on one last round of IVF, post that, they would visit a surrogacy agency if needed. And while Nikki hoped the IVF treatment would work, and she would get pregnant, it didn't.

'I'm going for a run. I'll call Eira and tell her about our baby plans today,' Nikki said, shrugging into her hoodie jacket.

'Be kind to yourself.' Sai reminded her as she bent down to tie her bright pink laces.

'I will.' Nikki flashed a thumbs-up sign and wrapping her headphones around her neck she closed the door behind her.

'Yo. What's shaking?' Eira asked, with midweek cheer, while steering her car carefully into the parking space at work. 'I got called in for an unscheduled meeting, so you've got about ten minutes to speak while I make my coffee and settle in because then, Gina the destroyer of my peace arrives. You're on the clock. Your time starts now.'

'I have news.'

'You're pregnant? Holy mother of—'

'No, *No.*' Nikki clicked her teeth, irritation twirling in her voice. 'I'm going to Mumbai next month.'

'Oh yes, you mentioned it earlier, for Dhruv's fortieth, right?'

'His birthday is one of the reasons.' Nikki found a spot in the shade of a large willow tree and sat down to catch her breath. After a three-mile run, her heart rate was now at 187 beats per minute.

'One of the reasons?' Eira parroted. 'What's the other reason?'

'You know how unsuccessful we've been with our baby making skills. I've done hormones, injections, IVF, and here I am – *still* not pregnant. God alone knows how much Sai and I have tried. It's as if my ovaries are plotting against me, and I hate that stupid "don't stress yourself out when you're trying to conceive" advice. How is it possible to stay calm after all that scheduled-in-sex and no positive results to show? How? I don't get it.' Nikki sucked in a deep breath. 'So, we're now considering surrogacy. I'm going to meet the head of *New Life*—a surrogacy agency in Manhattan that Sai's colleague recommended—and discuss our case. I'm told they have a very high pregnancy success rate.' She paused. 'Interesting name for a surrogacy agency, *hai na*?'

Eira didn't know what to say to make her feel better. Nikki loved children, and she was great with them. Zasha adored her aunt, and not just because she was hip and tech-savvy and sported a tattoo sleeve on her right arm. Nikki was a no-nonsense person like her. They said it the way they felt it. Zasha never had to worry about Nikki mincing her words. Depriving Nikki of a child was probably the nastiest joke God had played on her.

'Is this what you want to do?' Eira asked.

'What I want is a child of my own; a big bulge with a tiny human growing inside of me. I want to feel those rhythmic kicks of a baby that mothers go goo-goo-gaga over. I want that disgusting heartburn and burps, and I want to have food cravings. I want all of it, the whole package. But the shitty truth is: I can't. I never will. So, if this is the only way I will hold a child of my own in my arms, then yes, *hell yes,* this is what I want.' Nikki leaned against the deeply fissured bark of the old tree. 'This is our last attempt at becoming parents, or else I'm going to have to be content with playing second mommy to Zasha. I'm done here.'

'I thought India passed a new bill banning NRIs and foreigners from using Indian women as surrogates?'

'I heard the same. But I'm not going to India to find a match. I need some finances and paperwork to be sorted out.'

'*Acha* got it. Honey it's going to work out just fine.' Eira attempted to sound positive about the surrogacy. 'Don't let a few setbacks deflate your enthusiasm to have a baby. Be hopeful.'

'I don't know how Sai puts up with me anymore—I've driven him crazy with all this pregnancy BS.' Nikki said as a steady flow of tears rolled down her cheeks and dissolved into her sweat. 'Both of us love children, and I feel as if I am cheating him out of that wonderful experience.'

'Nikki, go easy on yourself. Sai isn't with you for a baby. He's been in love with you since you guys were nineteen, and nothing, *absolutely* nothing has changed. He seems as besotted with you as he did fifteen years ago. If a child was a binding factor wouldn't I be with Dhruv today? Believe me, when I say this, Sai's stuck to you like glue because he loves you truly, madly, deeply.'

'Okay, that last sentence was corny.' Nikki smiled, wiping away her smudged mascara with the edge of her thumb.

'It made you smile, right? Then I don't mind being a corny fart.'

'You're like my pocket fairy, sprinkling stardust over my crazy thoughts and helping me calm my nerves. Thanks babe. Anyway, so how's your vote-deciding dinner preparations coming along? Need some help? I can still come over.'

'You can't fry an egg. How are you going to help?' Eira quipped, as she thumbed through the latest issue of the Architectural Record.

'I wasn't offering my culinary skills, smart ass. I can play referee between Zasha and your doctor.'

'I would love for you to meet Nihal, but not this time honey. I really want this to be as casual as possible. I don't want him to get intimidated.'

'Ya. Ya. I was just trying my luck. Keep me posted. I am excited for you, Eira. I really hope Zasha comes around.'

'Me too. Now you get back to galloping around Manhattan, and I'm going to look busy. Gina's here. Talk soon.'

Eira was not herself that day. She was disturbed by Nikki's confession of helplessness. It felt as if the universe was denying her the gift of motherhood and not allowing her to have a family she craved. It was all *so* terribly wrong. Nikki always managed to find a silver lining; even the darkest cloud wasn't left disappointed. She had stood by Eira and had been her pillar of strength all through her pregnancy, and in helping them relocate from New York too. She never allowed Dhruv to come in the way of their friendship. Eira relished the fact that they were friends before family, which is why they could skip all the familial politics. But this...*this* whole pregnancy thing was different. The harder she tried, the more it seemed to slip from her hand. Eira felt powerless about not being able to do anything for her best friend.

The next two days flew by like a Japanese Shinkasen—Eira was running on schedule, and there were no screw-ups—juggling work and organizing the best dinner she'd ever hosted. The cleaners had been called in a second time this month for Nihal didn't need to see their furniture filigreed with dust. Despite Eira's reluctance, her mother insisted on baking *Malva* pudding, a kind gesture to incorporate his South African heritage. Going by past results, Eira hid a tub of chocolate and mint ice-cream at the back of the freezer as an emergency dessert. Zasha had been uncommonly quiet, no wisecracks or below the belt comments, she'd even helped with setting the table and taking out the trash. Her sudden change in behaviour seemed suspect.

'It's 6.30? Where's your guest, Eira?' Kanika asked, adjusting the dial on her wrist.

'He's a doctor, Nani. He saves lives. Although, he needs to get to the patient on time.' Zasha replied. There it was, the first gibe for the evening.

'Nihal will be here in five, Mummy. He had to make a quick stop at the gas station to fill fuel.' Eira ignored Zasha's sarcasm and continued replying to emails on her phone. When the minute hand grazed seven on her diamond-studded Kenneth Cole, Eira heard his car pull into their driveway. Her head felt light and fear sloshed around inside her like squishy pieces of mango in a Magic Bullet blender. This evening had to be perfect for both Nihal and Zasha. They had to like each other.

Kanika jumped to her feet when she heard the rap on the door. She wanted to be the first person to greet her future son-in-law.

Chapter Nine

'Good Evening, Mrs Dey.' Nihal greeted Kanika, handing her a bunch of sunny yellow tulips in a nest-like woven basket. He scanned the room for Eira, and when his eyes found hers, he felt a sea of relief wash over him. Zasha took the flowers from her grandmother and placed the basket on the little repurposed wooden table in the foyer.

'You don't have to take off your shoes. It's fine,' Kanika offered, seeing Nihal bend down to unlace his shoes so that he could place them on the doormat.

'Oh. My mother would never allow us into the living room with our shoes. It's just a habit now. If that's okay with you? I feel more comfortable with them off.'

'As you wish.' Kanika smiled.

When Zasha returned, Eira proceeded to introduce Nihal to her, but her daughter initiated her own introduction. 'Hi, I'm Zasha, the daughter. I'm sure you've heard a lot about me.'

'Pleased to meet you, Zasha.' Nihal shook her hand; her grip was strong and purposeful. 'Eira never stops singing your praises.' He smiled with breezy confidence.

That was the first cross on Zasha's list. She just didn't buy it.

'Really, like what?' Zasha knit her fingers carefully around her knees.

'For starters, you are a fantastic goalie. Eira's supremely proud of your soccer skills, and I've seen a few of your charcoal paintings, they're not brilliant, but they're good.' Ah, some honesty, a breath of fresh air. Zasha appreciated his *not brilliant* comment.

'Funny, I haven't heard plenty about you.' Zasha smirked. 'Do you play a sport?' Zasha quizzed him.

'Not anymore. I don't have the time to play a sport; although, I do try to catch a good baseball game whenever I can.' Nihal's gaze shifted to Kanika who was staring at his feet.

'Everything okay, Mrs Dey?'

'You have large feet,' she blurted, looking around the room hoping the others had noticed them too.

'I am a tall man, Mrs Dey.' Nihal smiled, amused by her observation.

'True.' Kanika nodded. 'And you can call me by my first name,' she added.

'Kanika it is then.'

'Who's thirsty?' Eira jumped in. 'There's white wine and beer or water too.'

'A beer for me.' Nihal raised his arm.

'I'll get that.' Kanika offered and made her way to the kitchen.

'Come, see the rest of our home.' Eira jumped up from the couch and took Nihal by the arm. She wanted to give him a few tips, the first one being no more comments on Zasha's achievements. Second, no discussion about her school progress, and third, no conversation that led to Dhruv or Shikhar.

'I love your home. It's so cosy.' Nihal said running his palm over the hand-carved, cedar wood dresser.

'You mean it's small and crowded?'

'And you wonder where your daughter gets her haughtiness from?' Nihal teased. 'I really like the style. It's a home. I want one like this with you,' he said, with an earnest look in his eyes.

'Nihal, let's get through this evening first.' Eira twiddled with the moisturizer tube on her dresser.

'And if I don't get your daughter's stamp of approval?'

'Nihal, can we please discuss this later. I know she is not being easy. But Zasha is a teenager who's, unfortunately, dragging her mother's baggage.'

'Okay. Fine. Let's hope she gives me a chance to show her I'm a decent guy and that I love you.' He drew her close to him and gave her a light peck on her cheek.

'We should head back to the living room before they come up here.' Eira held out her hand and led him downstairs.

Nihal had made a good first impression on Kanika. He was polite and soft-spoken, and what she appreciated most about him was that he was a good listener. He was in no rush to talk about himself. He regaled her with colourful stories about his childhood visits to South Africa, and she shared stories about her work trips to different countries of the African continent. She was delighted to know he had spent a year in Tanzania working on the ground with a local NGO in their community clinic. Nihal was easy going and had no air about his accomplishments. Unlike Shikhar, he wasn't a silver-tongued orator, and he certainly didn't wear his success on his sleeve.

'Nihal, if I may ask, are you a Trump supporter?' Zasha spat out a question that had been chewing her insides all evening.

'Zasha, we're not discussing politics tonight, and I'm sure Nihal's not keen on discussing it too.' Kanika knew this was not an innocuous question; in fact, it was a leading one.

'I'm not a Trump supporter,' Nihal replied.

'There, happy?' Eira shook her head delighted by his response.

'But I am Republican,' Nihal continued. Eira looked up from her beer in disbelief. *Why would he do that? Why couldn't he just stick to the question being asked*, she thought.

'Oooh. Mom, did you hear that?'

'And you already knew that because you looked me up and watched my interview on CNN. Am I right?'

'I did my homework,' Zasha snorted. 'So, are you Pro-Life or do you believe in a woman's right to choose?' Zasha aimed a carefully loaded question at Nihal, and well expected it to put him in a tight spot.

'I am a doctor. I save lives. I know when an abortion is a medical necessity.' Nihal replied with confidence, hoping his answer had cleared her doubts.

'Just asking, if my mother didn't keep me and chose an easier option instead, would you support her choice?'

Eira's heart plummeted. 'Zasha, I don't think this is an appropriate topic of discussion.' She was embarrassed by her daughter's brashness.

'It's okay. I'm glad we're having an open conversation,' Nihal said, turning his attention towards Zasha once again, 'I respect your mother for having you. It takes a lot of courage to do the right thing. Hope that answers your question.'

And just like that, a dark cloud lifted from above Eira's head. His thoughts were out there. Up until then, Eira hadn't realized how much Nihal's acceptance of her as a single parent had meant to her. But why did it matter? It didn't bother her when she was with Shikhar. Something about Nihal made her want to be perfect, when in fact he was in love with all her flaws.

'Do you want kids…your own family?' Zasha was unstoppable.

'That's enough. Nihal isn't here for an interrogation.' Eira turned towards Nihal and nodded her head from side to side to ignore Zasha's question. She wasn't mentally prepared to hear what he had to say. They hadn't talked about more children. Eira didn't want any surprises.

Nihal spent the rest of the evening talking about his med school days and some of the recent breakthroughs in medical science. Kanika was intrigued by some of the cases he shared with her. Zasha was quiet through the dinner, hoping her silence would make him uncomfortable.

'I love this pudding.' Nihal scooped a spoonful into his mouth.

'You do?' Kanika's eyes brightened. 'I looked it up on the Internet.'

'What is this dessert called?'

'Malva pudding, a South African delicacy.' Kanika frowned. 'You've never eaten it before?'

'I may have tried it...but this is yum!' Nihal said, sensing the disappointment in Kanika's eyes. 'My mother has limited culinary skills; she stuck to a few recipes that she knew best. Please don't tell her I told you.' Nihal eased up, his eyes crinkling at the corners.

'That makes two of us. Eira, on the other hand, is a great chef.'

'I take after Dad. Although I love my spices, and Dad was more of an herb person, remember Mummy?' Eira said, waiting for her mother to endorse her observation. But Kanika was silent.

'Mummy?'

'Yes. Yes. You're like your father,' Kanika faltered.

'I live off hospital food, so for me, a simple home-cooked meal is a big deal. Sometimes I think Yolo eats healthier than me.'

'Who's Yolo?' Kanika asked.

'My German Shepherd. He's a good dog.'

Zasha's face lit up when she heard he had a canine friend. She loved dogs, but Eira was clear they couldn't keep a dog, while they lived on rent. She would consider a pet when they moved into their own home.

'I prefer cats,' Kanika said. 'But dogs are fun to have too.'

'May I be excused?' Zasha cut in. 'I have a ton of schoolwork to finish and a Spanish test coming up too.' A perfectly believable excuse she thought.

'It's a long weekend.' Kanika replied. 'And you haven't finished your dessert.'

'It's okay Mummy, Zasha you can go upstairs.' Eira conceded. There was no point in forcing Zasha to get to know Nihal. Her daughter had a mind of her own, and she wouldn't budge. This was going to take more than one dinner.

'Good Night everyone.' Zasha left the table, careful not to make eye contact with Nihal. It was her way of showing him she disapproved.

'Just a thought. What do you guys think about getting away from the city and driving to Peaks of Otter, say a month from now?' Nihal asked, dabbing off the latte foam that spread to the outer reaches of his mouth. 'Zasha will be off school. I think she will love the place. My folks live there, and I'm sure they would be happy to meet you ladies.'

Kanika hesitated. It was a lovely opportunity to meet his parents, but Eira had to be comfortable with the idea first.

'Not so soon.' Eira squared her shoulders. 'Zasha needs more time.'

'Sure. I get it. Let me know whenever.' Nihal eased back into the vintage rocking chair that Eira had inherited from her maternal grandmother, a few of the things they had shipped to the US when they sold off their house in Chittaranjan Park.

It could have been worse, Eira thought as she escorted Nihal to his car. 'I'm sorry about tonight. I thought I raised her better.' She sighed.

'You're a good mother. Don't ever question that. I'm in no rush for her to accept me. I'm here for the long haul.' He smiled. 'I love you.' Nihal kissed her on the cheek. 'Your daughter's watching from upstairs. I better behave. Cya.'

Eira stood on the street and watched his car disappear in the dark. Her mind flipped ahead to the weekend getaway to Peaks of Otter. Nihal wanted her to meet his parents. What did this mean? Was he going to propose soon? No. But he had just said he was in no rush. Did his parents know she was a single mother? Were they aware of Dhruv's presence in her life? What about Shikhar! If they did, did they believe she had no part to play in the fraud? Multiple unrelated thoughts swirled around in her head. She would have to meet them to know how they felt about her. Soon, she thought.

When Eira went back inside the house Kanika was packing up the leftovers.

'I like him,' Kanika said, pinching the plastic lid to the sides of the red Tupperware bowl.

'Me too.' Eira smiled, sponging off the kitchen counter with lemon spray. 'But I can't guarantee him a future together.'

'A little too late, don't you think? He's completely into you.'

'You're a hoot. Where did you learn that line?'

'Jennifer Anniston.' Kanika smiled sheepishly.

'I want to be with him too, but I'm on shaky ground with Zasha.' Eira flicked her eyes upward and let out a steady stream of air. 'Mummy, I want to thank you for encouraging me to take this step.'

'You knew what you had to do. You just needed a little push. I hope you'll find a way to make this work for the three of you.' Kanika patted her on the cheek. 'Good night. Sleep well. A little piece of advice, don't talk to Zasha about this dinner yet. Give her a couple of days—she will definitely talk to Mia about it—and that's okay.'

The weekend stretched, and for the first time, Eira wished she was back at the office. That way she didn't have to deal with Zasha's silent treatment. Eira was itching to ask her daughter what she thought about Nihal, but she was also anxious about the response. If Zasha made a list of pros and cons, which was not something she would do, but if she did, Eira was pretty sure, Nihal scored more negatives on it. Was there anything…just anything that Zasha liked about him? If only she could crawl inside her daughter's head, she wouldn't have to drive herself crazy with all the *ifs* and *buts*.

'Why didn't you call me yesterday?' Nikki demanded. 'I was waiting to hear all about your big dinner.'

'Because I was playing cat and mouse with Zasha. And a part of me was hoping she would say something positive so that I could give you some good news.'

'Which means it went all wrong?'

'I wouldn't go that far, but what do you do when your boyfriend confesses he's a Republican supporter right in front of the country's most loyal Democrat.'

'Whoa.' Nikki tried to contain her laughter, but her amusement was evident through the phone. 'We're finally calling Nihal your boyfriend now.'

'Really, you think *thaaat* is funny?'

'Kinda.'

'I know he's too old to be calling him my boyfriend, but I don't know what else to call him.'

'It's so easy to set you off, isn't it?' Nikki giggled. 'Coming back, how did you not know his political allegiance? I mean…he is half black, half brown.'

'Ah, the cliché, minorities vote for the Democrats. I'm ashamed of you my friend.' Eira paused. 'Truth be told, I knew.'

'Wow. This guy is something else. He's got you, babe.'

'He hasn't got me around his finger or anything like that. He's simply different from my previous choices. I told you that before.'

'Your choice in men isn't consistent. I don't see a definite pattern.'

'This is only my second substantial relationship if you don't count Dhruv, so—'

'Well, good luck with your Republican.'

'I need a lot of that. Gotta go. Talk soon.'

Tuesday took a long time to come around, but when it did, Eira was pleased as punch to have her schedule chock-a-block for the next few days. It didn't give her any time to cook up stories and drive herself nuts. Plus, it was good to look busy a week before the appraisal meeting. Gina would be more inclined to seal the deal on her promotion. Eira spent her evenings clicking links to houses on the market forwarded by a real estate agent who came highly recommended by Nihal. He'd bought his home using this agent's services, and even though she had more realtor contacts through her own network in the construction industry, Eira went ahead with Nihal's recommendation.

Chapter Ten

'Thank you, God. Thank you. Thank you.' Eira shrieked into the phone.

'You're religious now?' Nihal laughed.

'Oh, I am super pleased with the Divine One today. Say hello to the new Project Manager at TJ Ellipse. Ta da.' Eira was beaming with excitement. In her head, she was already packing boxes and hiring movers.

'This calls for a celebration. Where are you taking me? I hope you've realized we haven't seen each other in two weeks, not since that rapid-fire Q&A at your home.'

'There...I was waiting for that. I knew you were keeping the truth from me.'

'Ha ha,' Nihal chortled. 'I was trying to be funny. I thought it went well. Kanika is a delight, and your daughter is fiery and extremely passionate about her beliefs, but it's a good thing. She takes after you.'

'Are you still doing the polite thing?'

'No. I don't have kids of my own, but I interact with them and their parents nearly every day. Zasha is a good kid; *she is simply looking out for both of you. She doesn't want to see you hurt.'*

'Me, hurt?'

'Yes. She is doing the interrogation for both of you. Zasha doesn't trust your decision-making anymore. She's taken it upon herself to do that for you. Zasha is far more mature for her age. I guess her male interactions with other men in your life may have something to do with it, but let's not get into that discussion right now. Let's celebrate your success today. I'll swing by for lunch tomorrow. I'll pick the place this time, and you get to treat me. Sound good?'

'Sure.' Eira was distracted and ended up committing to a Saturday lunch. Her thoughts lingered on Nihal's observation; *she is simply looking out for both of you.* Is that what Zasha was doing? Had she scarred her daughter for life? Was Zasha hoping Dhruv and she would get together, or did she not want any man in their life? It was time to talk to her about Nihal—no more sweeping her feelings for Nihal under the carpet—but not tonight. It could wait one more day. Today was about celebrating her hard work and perseverance, and how close she was to her dream of owning a home. She could now design a real study for herself instead of the pokey basement space she was currently using. Kanika could also go all out with her gardening plans; they could even bring in a professional landscaper. Zasha, of course, would be only too pleased to know she could have a larger space for her art. But the first thing on Eira's list of must-haves was a larger kitchen. She was looking forward to baking more on the weekends. Cooking was therapeutic for her. One night during Shikhar's trial case she baked a hundred and fifty muffins and then shared them in the office the next day. Her colleagues thought she had gone crazy—who distributes muffins when their lover is on the brink of being convicted? But Eira had to bake to release her stress. Baking was her thing, so when her mother insisted on the Malva pudding she felt robbed of her stress buster, but she had to pick her battles, *argue with her mother a night before or go for the next best substitute, a bar of Twix*. Nerves-a-jangle that night it took her two bars of the biscuity chocolate and a slice of a day-old banana bread to decompress.

But today she was standing at the doorstep of a bright future that she had worked for tirelessly. She could now begin her house tour in the Alexandria waterfront area; those red brick houses with tree-lined streets is what she had her eyes on for the last nineteen months, which also meant they would be moving state. It was clear if she was ever going to be a homeowner, she had to move out from downtown D.C. and into a suburban Alexandria, and Zasha would have to live with that.

On her way home, to mark the occasion, Eira picked up a tub of Ben and Jerry's and a bottle of Bret Brothers finest chardonnay. An occasion like this called for an upgrade from her twelve-dollar regular Prosecco.

'Hello, anyone home?' Eira called out from the foyer. She dumped a sheaf of mail in the wicker catchall by the door and proceeded to put the ice-cream tub in the freezer.

'Hey, what are you doing? You guys had dinner without me?' Eira asked, eyeing Zasha's bowl.

'It's movie night Mom. We ordered the pizzas. I didn't want to get up in the middle of the movie, so I made us some popcorn too.' Zasha replied, loading her bowl with caramel popcorn in the kitchen.

'Shoot, I forgot. Which movie are we watching?'

'*Raees*. It's Nani's night, and she picked Bollywood.' Zasha replied, plucking a paper towel to clean up the bits that had fallen on the counter. 'I have something to tell you, Mom.'

'I have some news too. I'm going to take a shower. I'll be with you guys in fifteen minutes. Wait for me. Oh, and I bought Chunky Monkey for dessert.'

'The best flavour after a cheesy pizza.' Zasha sounded cool as if nothing was wrong between them.

Twenty minutes later, dressed in her favourite tattered orange shorts, Eira stood before the television set, blocking the paused screen. Kanika eyed her over the rimless spectacles that she picked up in India last summer. 'You want to say something?'

'Ok, here it is. We're going to be moving soon. I got the promotion, and I'm a Project Manager now.' Eira announced with a dramatic flourish.

'Well done darling.' Kanika rose from the couch to give her daughter a hug, but Eira's eyes were fixed on Zasha, who seemed preoccupied with other thoughts.

'Aren't you happy? You can have more space.'

'Yea. Congrats Mom,' Zasha said half-heartedly. 'So, when do we go house hunting?'

'Soon. You have two more weeks of school. So, after that.'

'Yea about that, I won't be here for the summer holidays.'

'What do you mean?'

'I spoke to Dad, and he said I could spend the holidays with him in India. He'll pay for the ticket.'

'When did you speak to Dhruv?' Despite her best intentions, Eira found herself losing her cool.

'A week ago. He said I had to clear it with you myself. I didn't think it would be a problem. It's his 40th birthday, and I thought he would appreciate having his daughter around.'

Eira licked her lips counting silently to ten. 'And you realized it was his 40th birthday a week ago?'

'What are you hinting at?'

'You know what I'm talking about.' Eira turned towards the television as tears swam in her eyes. This was supposed to be her day. Her moment. And it had been taken away from her like many others. 'You're going to travel by yourself?'

'No. Dad said Nikki aunty is travelling to Mumbai too, and he would ask her to travel with me. He'll figure that out once you approve.'

'Did you tell him about Nihal, if I may ask?'

'In bits.'

'It wasn't your news to share.' Eira was red in the face now.

'I didn't tell him I hate him, just that you have a new boyfriend,' Zasha snapped.

'How long will you be gone?'

'A month, or whatever you're fine with.'

'Okay. I'll talk to your dad tomorrow.' Eira ran her hand through her hair. 'I'm not feeling too good; you guys continue with movie night.'

She cut a slice of pizza and took it up to her room. She was pissed off with Zasha for plotting behind her back, but she was even more disappointed with Dhruv for not telling her about Zasha's plans. They had agreed on some rules on co-parenting. She felt blindsided. He was playing good cop when they'd promised to never turn against each other. He was punishing her for not letting them be a family. It was always part of his plan to strike when the iron was hot. How could he? Just because he was miserable after losing his wife, he was trying to ruin it for her too, Eira thought. She wasn't going to take this lying down. She planned to give him a piece of her explosive mind, but only after she had spoken to his sister. Was Nikki in the loop too?

'Hey, babe. Congratulations on the promotion. I'm so proud of you. What are you doing tonight? Where are the celebrations?' Nikki asked.

'Did you know Zasha—'

'Hold on. The network is terrible in this room.' Nikki picked up her night read and shuffled from the den to the living room. 'Sorry, you were saying?'

'Nikki, have you spoken to Dhruv lately?'

'Not this week, why?'

'Did you know Zasha was planning a trip to India?'

'No. I am the cool aunt, but she knows not to tell me stuff like that. I wouldn't keep those details from you.' Nikki's eyebrows furrowed. 'Did you think I would go behind your back?'

'I don't know what to think anymore.'

'For starters, you can trust the people you say you love.' Nikki hated being doubted.

'I'm sorry. It's just one thing after another in this house. I didn't go out for drinks with Nihal or my colleagues and came straight home to share my win with my daughter and my mother. And somehow, she has bigger news for me. She told me she wants to go to Mumbai for Dhruv's birthday and spend a month there. And Dhruv said yes. Can you believe that? Oh, and this takes the cake, she told him that I have a new boyfriend.'

'So which part's bugging you more, the part that he knows you're seeing Nihal or the part where he said yes to his daughter's request to spend time with him.'

'I see what you're doing.'

'What am I doing?'

'You're doing the whole answer your own questions nonsense.'

'Maybe. And what do you think is bugging you more.' Nikki asked, cradling the cordless phone between her ear and cheek while she typed a stern message to Dhruv on her cell phone – *What the hell? When did you decide Zasha was travelling with me?*

'One month. A whole month of summer. It's a long time. I don't think she will be fine on her own.'

'You mean you don't think you will be fine on your own, because she has her father to look out for her.'

'Okay, whose side are you on, Nikki?'

'I'm not taking sides. Dhruv is my brother, and you are family too. I never have and never will choose between the two of you. But you're sounding a little unfair. He has a right to spend time with his daughter, and she is old enough to travel on her own now. Besides, you have Nihal. Dhruv's still recovering from the loss of his wife. It's only been fifteen months, that's not a lot of time. I'm sure his daughter's presence would help him move forward. Don't you think so?'

'Okay fine. I'm not pissed off with Dhruv. Besides, he did tell her she had to clear it with me first. But I can be mad at Zasha. She is just doing this to annoy me.'

'A little distance might help you two, think about it.'

'What if she decides to stay back with Dhruv? I know this sounds horrible, and while I genuinely thought Dhruv's wife was a really lovely woman...with her no longer in the picture, what if Zasha considers living with him? What will I do?'

'Eira, stop panicking. Nothing of that sort is going to happen. Dhruv won't allow it. Give him some credit. He's a good father, and he knows you're a fantastic mom. Have some faith in the people who love you.'

'What's with the trust and faith talk today? Can't you just agree with me?'

'If I can have faith and trust that the surrogate will get pregnant and allow me to have a child I have been longing for, I'm sure you can have a little faith in your child that she loves you and will come back to you, after a fun-filled holiday with her father. Now don't overthink the situation and get to bed. Tomorrow's a new day with its own set of surprises. I love you. Don't be mad at me, but sometimes you are a little crazy.'

'Love you too and stop obsessing about the surrogacy. It will work out just fine.'

That week, Eira and Dhruv ironed out the finer details about their daughter's solo trip to India. While Zasha would travel to India with her aunt, Dhruv agreed to fly back with her since Nikki had only planned a 15-day trip. This way, Zasha didn't have to travel by herself. They agreed on a month-long stay, and he promised he would ensure Zasha spoke to Eira every day. Dhruv didn't bring up Nihal in any of their conversations. There was no need to pry. He knew Eira well enough, and she would talk about something or someone only when she was ready.

Two weeks passed faster than Eira imagined, and she was now standing at the departure gates waiting to hug her daughter goodbye before she could take off for Mumbai. Eira and Zasha were both playing it cool and hiding their anxiousness – this was a gigantic step for both, a month that had the potential to change several lives.

With Zasha away, Nihal was agog about spending more time with Eira. He had all four weekends planned out. On the other side, Kanika was hopeful about this month too. *Maybe Eira and I could use this time to smoothen out our own differences too*, she thought.

Chapter Eleven

'I know the list by heart: no flunky haircuts, no body piercings especially diamond nose studs by the grandmother, no temporary hair colour, no travelling by domestic transport by herself, no tiny sips of beer. This last one I can't guarantee you. We're Punjabis, we love our *daaru*. She might land up having her first brush with alcohol with us, just a tiny sip to christen her into the Kapur *khaandan*.' Nikki winked unapologetically. 'Did you give Dhruv the same list?'

'His list covers a different set of topics. I know he will go overboard since it is the first time Zasha is spending a month with him, and it is perfectly normal for him to feel overwhelmed by the attention. However, in a month, she's back to frugal living, and I don't want to have to deal with how great her father is and all the stuff he buys her that I don't. So, his list is more about controlling his purse. I trust him completely not to lead her to a hair salon. He's much more possessive about his little girl. You're the cool aunt, hence the list.'

'Aah, I see. What about the flight? Can I slip her a little red wine if she gets bothersome?' Nikki's recently plucked eyebrows rose like little peaks. 'Relax, I ain't going to ruin your daughter. Now get going, we have a flight to take.' Nikki wrapped her arms around her friend engulfing her in a reassuring hug. Eira turned around to embrace her daughter who still had her earphones tucked snug in her ears.

'Oi,' Nikki whacked her boarding pass on Zasha's head. 'Time to go.' Zasha looked up from her phone, and gauging by the look on Eira's face she knew it was time for goodbyes.

'Have fun, sweetheart. I'll miss you.' Eira squeezed Zasha in her arms. 'Always remember, Mom loves you, no matter what. Okay?'

'I love you too, Mom. Don't get into trouble,' Zasha said, only half believing that her mother would take her advice seriously.

'You too.' Eira forced a twisted smile and kissed Zasha on her forehead one last time. Eira watched her daughter wheel her steel grey carry-on until she slowly disappeared into the crowd. As she drove back home, her calm was replaced by familiar anxiety. The *Xanax* she had popped earlier that day was wearing off. This wasn't the summer she had in mind. Zasha and she were supposed to go to Yellowstone National park and marvel at geyser eruptions, pitch their tent on one of the twelve campgrounds and roast marshmallows, and hike along the Mystic Falls trail. Zasha had done most of the homework for this trip. They were just waiting for Eira's promotion to make the necessary reservations. Zasha had even made a compelling argument on why Mia and her mother should be part of their trip. And even though Eira hated the thought of spending the summer—the only time of the year they took a vacation—with Mia, she had agreed. Then how did everything go so wrong? Her tummy felt as if it was on tumble dry. Eira felt the beginnings of a migraine: a shooting pain in her temples that was slowly moving down to the lower part of her head. Her face felt fuzzy and tingly, and black and white circles swarmed her eyes distorting her vision. Eira crouched down to draw a bottle of water out of the bag resting at her foot. A drink of water always helped.

When Eira got home that afternoon, she was overcome by overbearing loneliness. Zasha had only been to two sleepovers, and that was two houses away. If there was a problem, she could just run over to Mia's house in the middle of the night to fetch her daughter. This new freedom felt so fragile.

Eira heard a jangle of keys and quickly wiped away the tears that had smeared her cheeks.

'What are you doing home?' Kanika asked in surprise. She'd assumed Eira would drive over to Nihal's place and spend the rest of the day with him.

'This is my home, where else would I go?' Eira snapped.

'Did something happen between you and Zasha?' Kanika placed her grocery bags on the kitchen counter and pulled a stool to sit down.

'Mummy—'

Kanika slid slowly off the stool and turned to leave when Eira held her hand. 'I'm sorry. I feel so dejected right now. I miss her already, and she didn't have even an iota of sadness in her eyes. I'm miserable.'

'You should go and meet Nihal. He will cheer you up.'

'No. She would hate it if she knew I went to meet him the moment she took off.'

'She also knew you would hate it if she went to spend the summer with her father.'

'She knew it, right?' Eira said, tears pooling in her eyes.

'But Zasha did what she had to, and the distance is good for both of you to see things with unfogged glasses. So, don't beat yourself unnecessarily, and instead, make the best of this month. It's the weekend, go out tonight. Don't worry about me. I'll order some pizza and watch an old *Amitabh* movie in peace without the two musketeers picking on my movie taste.'

'You have your evening planned out.' Eira sniffled and let a small smile escape her lips.

'We're child-free for a whole month. What's not to be excited about! You take it easy. Zasha is with her father, and he is a responsible one. She's coming right back here, and your next break may only be when she leaves for college.'

'Thanks, Mummy. Are you sure you'll be fine with both of us not around?'

'Go get a life. Isn't that what Zasha would tell us? Now stop worrying about your mother and disappear before I change my mind.' Kanika got busy putting the groceries away whistling a merry tune.

Nihal was peeping outside his window for the fourth time in seven minutes when the delivery boy finally parked his worn-out bike in the driveway. Dangling four Styrofoam boxes in a plastic bag, he made his way to the door, and just when he lifted an arm to press the doorbell a box of *raita* tumbled out and landed on the floor spilling out the contents on Nihal's doormat. The teenager was in complete panic mode. He apologized profusely for his clumsiness and even offered to help Nihal clean up the mess. Nihal was tempted to take him up on the offer but declined half-heartedly and hotfooted inside the house to set the food in the bowls. This was their first Saturday night together, and he wanted it to be nothing less than perfect. Mutton Dum Biryani now minus the *raita*, chicken tikka, chole bhature and gulab jamun for dessert. One could never go wrong with *Karim's* takeout. While the portions were generous, Karim was cautious about the oil in the food. The complimentary mouth-watering sweet *paan* he slipped in occasionally was to die for.

Nihal lit the lavender scented candle that he had purchased an hour ago from the local supermarket. He'd even changed the bed linen and tidied up the house in the best way he could. Eira had barely given him an hour's notice about her arrival.

At 6.03 p.m. Eira was at his doorstep, twelve minutes early, eating into his shower time. Nihal rushed to open the door his hair still wet and droplets of water running down his bare chest.

'Hey, you're early.' Nihal gave Eira a little peck on her cheek.

'And you greet all your visitors with this sexy look?'

'Nah. Only special ones who look like a million bucks.' He pressed his lips against hers this time and let his mouth linger on hers for a few seconds.

'Let's save some more of this for dessert.' Nihal hooked his arm around hers and led her to the living room. His stride had a new confidence, she noticed. It may have had something to do with the fact that they didn't have to hide their relationship anymore.

'You clean up well. The last time I was here—'

'I don't think I give you enough time to look around. We're too busy doing other stuff with the little time we have in hand.'

Eira blushed a shade of pink and took the glass of wine from his hand. She knew tonight would be no different and she didn't want it any other way. They had waited long enough to spend time together without any interruptions.

'Did you women cry at the airport?'

'I did, a little, but not enough to embarrass her.'

'How are you feeling?' Nihal perched himself on the couch by her side and slipped one arm around her.

'I've been better. By the way, it was my mother's idea that I should spend the evening with you.'

'Oh, so you weren't going to come over if she hadn't suggested it?'

'I was thinking about coming over tomorrow.' Eira batted her eyelashes playfully.

'And you're spending the night?'

'Of course, not. That's a bizarre suggestion.'

'Why?'

'Because.'

'Because what?' Nihal was mystified by her response. 'You're footloose.'

'Zasha ain't here, but my mother is…she won't say anything, but I can't.'

'We're in a relationship. You're a 34-year-old grown woman with a teenage daughter.'

'Okay. Can we not discuss this tonight? I'm happy to be here. I'll stay as long as you want me to, but I won't sleep the night. Not tonight at least, it's too soon. Baby steps please.'

'Whatever.'

'Please don't sulk. I'll make it up to you.' Eira gave him a coy look from under her freshly cut bangs.

'You bet you will.' A warm glow of love flooded his face. He unclipped her hair and let it tumble against her shoulders. Nihal bent his head and planted a hot kiss on her coralline-red lips slowly moving down to her neck. Eira's stomach clenched; she closed her eyes and let out a soft moan. He pressed her down on the couch and his mouth descended on hers once again. The contours of her body drove him wild, and he let his hands go rogue while allowing his whiskered cheeks to kiss every inch of her belly. In the dim lighting, he saw a glint of pleasure and contentment in her eyes; Eira's body moved in perfect rhythm with his. He felt her tremble under his weight. Nihal claimed every part of her body that evening, and they made love right there on his couch.

'I've got to take this call.' Eira untangled herself from his arms and wrapped the throw blanket that Nihal had used to hide a curry stain on the couch around her bare body.

'Who is it?' Nihal called after her.

'Dhruv,' she replied and disappeared into the kitchen.

When she returned, Nihal was still lying on the couch with his eyes shut. She tiptoed back to him and nestled in his arms in comfortable silence. Thirty minutes later, she woke up to a wet smushy feeling around her toes. Yolo was back from his doggy date; Nihal had sent him to a friend's place so they could have an uninterrupted tumble. Eira rubbed Yolo's ears and then patted the space next to her for him to join her on the couch. Yolo held up his neck for a little rub.

'Good boy, you're such a good boy.' Eira fussed over him and let him lick her all over her face.

'Why didn't you wake me?' Eira blinked with embarrassment. Nihal was dressed up and flipping through the sports channels on the television.

'Did you know you snore?'

'I do not.'

'Yes, you do. And there's nothing to be embarrassed about.'

'Okay enough. I'm hungry.'

'C'mere, you want to go again, you sexy vixen.' He leaned in and tugged at the blanket still wrapped around her with a wicked grin.

'Err. I'd like to eat some biryani. I'm famished.' Eira slithered away from the couch careful not to let Yolo's teeth get hold of the blanket.

'Yes. Ma'am. All that lovemaking has given me a ravenous appetite too.' Nihal playfully patted her ample bottom.

Eira spent a few minutes breathing in the lingering scent of his skin before she stepped into the shower cubicle and let a hot spray of water trickle down her body. Her gaze bounced around his bathroom – from the bath curtain to his toothbrush holder down to the bath mat. Everything in his bathroom was either white or blue. She went through the cabinet above the wash basin and found a half-used bottle of Listerine, an electric shaver, dental floss and a nail cutter. Nihal was a man with basic possessions, and unknowingly, it was this very quality of his that was driving her to fall crazily in love with him.

'Do you want another glass of wine?' Nihal asked, as he helped himself to some biryani.

'Nope.'

'So, I was wondering…' Nihal said, voice lurching as it always did when he had to discuss a sticky subject, '…do you talk to Zasha's father regularly? As in, every week?'

'We make it a point to speak as often as we can, but not every week, more like fortnightly. He likes to be in the loop of what's going on in Zasha's life, and I think that's wonderful. Don't you?' Eira sensed some discomfort in Nihal's question.

'Yea, yea. Of course.'

'Is there something else you want to ask me?'

'Does Dhruv know about us?'

'Yes.' There was a pregnant pause. 'Zasha mentioned *us* to him when she was negotiating her trip to India.'

'But did you tell him that you're seeing someone?'

'Umm. We haven't got down to talking about you, yet. It has been a busy month.' Eira tried to sound as convincing as she could, but she knew she was failing miserably.

'No other reason?' He gave her the gimlet eye.

'None that I can think of.' Her gaze slid away from his. 'I'll tell him as soon as I get a chance.'

'Cool. Whenever you think best.' Nihal's voice was distant.

'Hey, I love you.' Eira grabbed his hand and entwined his fingers with his. 'Don't be like this. You have no reason to feel insecure or possessive. Dhruv and I have a daughter together, that's all. There will never be anything between us. It's weird for me to tell him I'm dating when he's still grieving his wife's loss. I know he will be supportive of my decision. He's a good guy, just not the guy for me. You're my guy.' Eira got up from her seat and perched herself on his lap.

'Alright.'

'Ruff. Ruff.' Yolo barked, tugging at Eira's jeans vigorously. He clearly wasn't ready to share Nihal just yet, and he wasn't ashamed to mark his territory.

Chapter Twelve

25 June 2017

'Hey, sweetheart. Did you have a pleasant flight?' Eira stifled a yawn. It was 11 a.m., and she was still in bed. Sleep-ins were uncommon in their household. Nihal had dropped her back around three, and she lay awake thinking about him for another hour or so, but Zasha didn't have to know all the details. *A tiny omission is not a lie,* Eira told herself.

'The layover sucked, but the service on both flights was grand. I watched movies for about seven hours and munched on all the goodies they served.' Zasha adjusted the time on her wrist watch to match the local time in Mumbai. 'What did you do?'

'Nothing fancy. I ate Biryani last night and missed you when I popped two gulab jamuns in my mouth in one go.'

'From Karim's?'

For a few seconds, cross-continental silence descended upon them. 'Yes.' Eira eventually replied, leaving out a tiny nugget of information: the delivery logistics.

'I'm not jealous. I will have my fill here.'

'Eat all you can.' Eira longed for Zasha to tell her she missed her, but she knew it was going to be a lengthy wait. Her daughter was still mad at her. 'Who came to pick you from the airport?'

'Dad.'

'Just Dad?'

'Yep.'

'Hmm. And what about the others, have they been good to you?'

'Mom, it has barely been thirty minutes since I got here. Dad insisted I call you before I do anything else. I'm gonna shower now and then meet *Daada-Daadi* downstairs. They invited me over for ice-cream. Supposedly, there's a family lunch in my name tomorrow. It's some public holiday, so all the Kapurs are congregating here to study the prodigal granddaughter species. I'll have to be on my best behaviour.'

'You'll be fine. They will love you. Now you push off and freshen up. Don't keep them waiting. I love you my baby girl.'

'Me too. Off topic, but I won't be telling Dad anything about Dr Zane. I know you will make the right decision.' With that last sentence, Zasha had ensured her mother knew that all was not okay between them. She was standing her ground and was not going to accept Nihal in her life.

'Good night, Zasha. Be safe and take care of yourself. I'll call you tomorrow. Say hello to everyone from me.'

Eira knew she had to tell Dhruv about Nihal sooner than she hoped. She had to get him to throw in his support before Zasha returned home. After the Shikhar debacle, Zasha was out of her depth, and Dhruv insisted on meeting the next man Eira dated. When he got married, he ensured Zasha and she were comfortable with his to-be wife. Luckily for him, his wife wasn't a fraud. She would invite them for lunches and short vacations together even before they had tied the knot. Zasha was very fond of Dhruv's wife and was distraught by her untimely death – her body was recovered a week after the plane crash.

Zasha scrambled through her bags to find the gifts Eira had sent for her grandparents. It had taken Eira seven years to get on Dhruv's mother's good side. Only when Dhruv got married did his mother become more accepting of Eira. The hope of having another grandchild who would be both geographically and emotionally closer to them flickered once again. Dhruv's wife got pregnant within five months of marriage, but had three miscarriages that followed. With Nikki having pregnancy trouble, Dhruv's mother resigned to her fate: Zasha was going to be the only grandchild with the Kapur DNA.

'Daadi, it's so nice to see you.' Zasha bent forward and touched her grandmother's feet for her blessings. On their flight to Mumbai, Nikki shared a few pointers that would let her earn brownie points with her grandmother and seeking her blessings was one of them.

Dhruv's mother immediately reached for Zasha's arms and embraced her instead. 'Look at you, all grown up. So womanly. Have you got your period?'

'Aiye. Aiye. Mummy don't be embarrassing,' Nikki dove in.

'What's embarrassing? Every girl gets her period. I can't ask Dhruv about this, can I? That would be more embarrassing.'

'Yes, Daadi, a few months ago.' Zasha replied, her skin burning a deep red. 'This is for you.' Zasha handed over a bag of goodies.

'Ah, here it is.' Dhruv's mother smiled holding up three tubes of foot cream. 'You still don't get this here. I've to depend on your mother for these.'

'Why didn't you tell me, Mummy? I could send you some,' Nikki asked

'Do you have any time for your mother? You only talk to your papa.'

'Oh, God. Here we go again. I don't play favourites. Just tell me you want something next time, alright?' Nikki blew her cheeks out.

'Where's Dadaji?' Zasha's eyes scanned the bar area for her grandfather.

'He's probably monitoring his shares. I don't know why he can't retire like other senior citizens in this country!' Dhruv's mother nodded her head in frustration. 'I'll go see where he is.'

'How did I do, Nikki aunty?' Zasha sighed with relief when her grandmother left the room.

'You were brilliant. It's scary how similar you and Eira are around my mother. Relax, don't be so wound up.'

'She asked me about my periods. I was hoping she doesn't ask me about my bra size next.'

'I thought she would.' Nikki roared with laughter. 'She might take you bra shopping; honestly, that's not the worst thing that could happen. She shops at Marks & Spencer for her lingerie.'

'Eww. I don't want to go innerwear shopping with my grandmother.'

'I went innerwear shopping with her.'

'Well, she is your mother, and you had no option.'

'As if you have an option.'

'I'll find a way to wriggle out of it.' Zasha patted Nikki's arm resting along the back of the sofa.

'Wriggle out of what?' Came a deep, baritone voice from behind them. 'And where's my only granddaughter hiding.' Dhruv's father pretended to look under the large dining table as if he were playing peekaboo with her just as he did when she was three.

'I'm here.' Zasha skipped towards him and sunk her head into his large chest. No feet touching this time. Zasha and her grandfather got on like a house on fire. Like Dhruv, he was an easy-going man.

They spoke twice a month, and he would fill her in on all his travels. Zasha hoped someday she could jet set around the world too. He kept a close eye on Zasha's education and insisted on sending her to private school from the eighth grade onwards. Eira didn't resist his offer. There was a trust fund set up in Zasha's name, and she could do with some financial help to see her daughter get a good education. But Eira insisted on paying a one- third of the fees which itself was a huge chunk of their yearly expenses. The timing for a change in school was perfect. Alexandria had wonderful private schools, and Zasha would not have much ground to put up a fight.

'I prefer chatting with you on video chat.' Dhruv's father said, pouring himself a seventeen-year-old single malt. 'You look much tinier on the screen, more like a little girl.'

'Heh heh. Weird perks of technology.' Dhruv slipped into the space between Zasha and Nikki, giving each of them a bowl of Natural's famous *sitafal* ice cream.'

'How's your mother? I haven't spoken to her in a while.' Dhruv's father uncrossed his legs and reached for the bag of presents Eira had sent.

'She got a promotion.' Zasha voice was decked with pride. 'She's doing well otherwise too.'

'She does work very hard. I've been tracking her work; she's definitely gifted.'

'How are you tracking her work?' Zasha sucked in a breath.

'I have friends, and they have their own network. The world's shrinking in more ways than you will ever realize.' Dhruv's father didn't think there was anything wrong in tracking Eira's life.

'Are you checking on her?' Disappointment slowly crept into Zasha's voice.

'No, but we have to be sure you'll are fine.' Dhruv's mother swam into the conversation. 'After all that's happened, we thought—'

'Mom's got everything under control. There's nothing to worry about. We've got each other's back.'

'Papa, what have you guys been doing?' Dhruv asked alarmed by his parents' comments.

'We're doing what's best for our granddaughter. What's the fuss about?'

'Guys it's Zasha's first night here, and you'll have already started the bickering. Give the child a break. Save it for after I'm gone.' Nikki jaws clenched with irritation.

'Dadaji, I'd like to come by your office one day, if that's okay with you?' Zasha attempted to change the subject to avoid an argument between her grandfather and Dhruv.

'Sure *sure*. You let me know when and I will block an hour to show you around.'

'No *office-shoffice* this week, beta. I want to take you to meet my friends, and we have our relatives coming over too.'

'Yes, Daadi. I'm all yours this week.'

'Nikki beta, take her to the gymkhana too. She will like it there.'

'But Daadi, I don't work out. What will I do at the gym?'

'*Arre baba*, it's not an exercise gym, although it does have a fitness centre. It's just nice to go play carrom or TT. They have a large pool too, although I will have to check if a member's guests can use the facility.'

'TT?'

'*Hai*, you're such an American. TT…table tennis.'

'She is American,' Nikki muttered.

'Yea, but she's acting like the *goras* now.'

'No Daadi, I'm a desi at heart.' Zasha tugged at her grandmother's cheeks. 'I'm waiting to eat yummy *gobi parathas*. Dad swears by your food.'

'Seriously? Your dad and aunt rarely ever compliment me. Good to know, if nothing else they at least like my food. Most days, I feel like an old lady whose children have flown the nest.'

'Oh Mummy, stop fishing. My nest is just two floors above yours, not too far. You come pecking every day.' Dhruv clapped his mother's arm playfully.

'They think I'm pecking at them.'

'Mummy, you are such a *nautanki*.' Dhruv rose from his seat and stretched his arms behind his back cracking his knuckles. '*Chalo* Zasha, it's late. Scoop up that last bit of ice-cream and let's call it a night.'

'See you in the morning, *Daada-Daadi*.' Zasha waved out to them and followed her father upstairs. Dhruv lived alone in an apartment two floors above his parents. There were two more Kapurs residing in the building with their families – his father's younger brothers. When Dhruv lost his wife, it had been nice to have his family so close to him, caring for his every need, reassuring him that life would get better again.

Zasha lay in bed, eyes wide open. She was on D.C. time. She tried reading a book to lull herself to sleep, but it didn't do the trick. She graduated to counting sheep, but after sixty-two, it felt lame. She turned and tossed like a Thai stir-fry in a wok. Twenty-five minutes later, Zasha threw off the duvet and stepped outside her room to see if anyone else was awake. Dhruv's snores penetrated through his bedroom walls. Zasha zipped open her bags and began unpacking. Her room felt as if no one had slept in it before. Even with all the classy furniture and 600-thread count, ivory-coloured, Egyptian cotton sheets, it felt bare. The room lacked warmth; it needed some colour. Zasha made a list of all the things she would need to make her room feel cosier. She planned to go to the local shops the next day and buy some of the stuff. One month was too long to live in a room that resembled a corporate hotel suite.

Downstairs, Nikki was having trouble sleeping too. A part of her wanted to go and check on Zasha, but she'd promised Dhruv she would let them have this time together, and even though she would have much rather stayed with her brother, she decided to stay downstairs with her parents. *Fifteen days will fly by*, Sai tried to convince her before he got off the call.

WhatsApp Chat

Nikki: Hey. I can't sleep

Eira: It's called jet lag. How did ice-cream with the grandparents go?

Nikki: No fireworks.

Eira: They love her. They reserve the fireworks for me.

Nikki: Mummy used to bitch about you, not anymore.

Eira: Thank you for the reminder.

Nikki: Lol

Eira: Is Zasha asleep?

Nikki: No clue. She hasn't messaged me to keep her company.

Eira: Me neither.

Nikki: That reminds me your daughter is like a hound when it comes to protecting you.

Eira: Why, what happened?

Nikki: Papa asked about you, to which she proudly shared your promotion news.

Eira: She did?

Nikki: Yea, and then when Papa told her that he kept checks on you to ensure you don't get into any trouble, she took up for you saying you guys have each other's backs. My heart jumped hearing that part. It was like music to my ears. Eira, our little girl's coming back.

Eira: One sec, what do you mean by your father checks on me?

Nikki: He likes to pretend like he's the CIA. Honestly, I don't think he's doing any such thing. It's just to keep my mother happy. She doesn't trust anyone.

Eira: Hmm. Actually, I don't care. I'm just happy my Zasha still thinks we're a team. I love that munchkin so very much. You tell her that. Also, please take care of my girl tomorrow; she mentioned a lunch or dinner that is being organized with the Kapurs.

Nikki: Of course, I will. How was your first night without Zasha?

Eira: I gotta dash. I'm taking my mother for a movie today. I'll message you later.

Nikki: Ok. Say hi to Kanika aunty for me. Ciao.

Chapter Thirteen

Zasha heard muffled voices from outside her door, which were followed by what sounded like a half tap.

'I'm awake.' She curled her nose: the smell of eggs and bacon had pervaded through the entire house. Sunny side up eggs, bacon, and avocado on toast was her favourite breakfast pick. In fact, she could eat bacon any time of the day; however, since her save-the-planet project Zasha had given up meat entirely.

'Oh good. Dhruv was acting crazy when I told him we should wake you up. I raced him to your door, and then he tried to tackle me, but I won, you woke up.'

'Such kids.' Zasha yawned. 'I was already up.'

'Then get your butt out from under those sheets and join me for my second breakfast.'

'What time is it?'

'Ten-ish.' Nikki drew the curtains.

'Good morning, honey.' Dhruv kissed her lightly on the forehead. 'Did you sleep well darling?'

'I think I dozed off around 2?'

'Eight hours is fantastic. I barely shut my eyes, and your grandmother had the cook grinding mint *chutney* at six bloody thirty. The melodious vrooms of the mixer grinder sounded like soft jazz to my ears.'

'You sound poetic, Nikki aunty.'

'Ignore her. She loves to exaggerate.' Dhruv said folding the crumpled duvet lying near Zasha's feet.

'What's this?' Nikki picked the list Zasha had drawn up. 'Wall decals, bed sheets, pillow covers, an easel stand and lights.'

'I was just thinking, maybe we could do up this room a little. It's a bit dull, as in…'

'Of course. I'll take you shopping tomorrow evening, and we will buy all the stuff you need.'

'Can't we just buy it off Amazon? They do a same-day delivery, and it might be cheaper too. Mom buys everything online…mostly.'

'Are you planning on staying back for more than a month?' Nikki's mouth twitched.

'No. I just want to make this feel a little bit like home. I miss my room, and if Dad doesn't want some of the stuff, I can take it back with me.'

Nikki's eyes fell on the photo frame poking out from under Zasha's pillow: a picture of Eira and her riding the roller coaster at Six Flags. Nikki's face softened. Zasha was probably homesick. It was her first time away.

'Dad, can you tell me who's going to be joining us for lunch today?' Zasha pushed the bacon with her knife to the far end of her plate hoping Dhruv wouldn't notice.

'Your Daadi's only sister and her daughter, and Dadaji's brothers, who live in this building. Their sons live with them, so they're going to be there too. One of my cousins have kids close to your age: Nikhil's thirteen and Pia's eleven, I think. So, you'll have company. The others are much younger.'

'And do they like us – Mom and me?'

'Don't be silly. Of course, they do.' Nikki pushed the bacon back to the centre of Zasha's plate. 'And just FYI, the only vegetarian food you're getting at today's lunch is *kachumber*. The carnivores will leap for the *roghan josht* and suck the marrow dry. You will offend the Kapurs if you pick on leaves.'

'But we should consider a root-to-stem food preparation. There are so many health benefits, and we can cut down on food wastage.'

'Root-to-wwwhat?' Nikki pulled a face. 'You better keep your vegetarianism on hold unless you want to spend an hour or more listening to my mother's take on why meat is the only healthy food on this planet. One more thing, don't roll your roti as if it's a sausage – dunk and chomp.'

'Dad,' Zasha purred.

'Nikki, stop hassling my daughter unnecessarily. Sweetie, just get through today's lunch. I will talk to my mother tomorrow. She will tell the cook to make something vegetarian for lunch, and I can cook your dinner.'

By noon, the first guest arrived. Dhruv's mother knew the Kapurs could never keep time, so she made sure her sister came earlier than the rest. This would give them exclusive time with Zasha. But her sister wasn't feeling too well, and instead of chatting with Zasha she spent fifty minutes talking about all the aches and pains in her body and the list of medicines the doctors had prescribed.

'Where are these people?' Nikki tutted disapprovingly at the clock. 'They just have to take the elevator upstairs. I need a drink. Let's crack open the new bottle I picked from duty- free.'

'You can't start drinking! The guests haven't even arrived,' Dhruv's mother scowled.

'But they should have been here by now.' Dhruv and Nikki said in unison.

'I'm not arguing with that logic.' Dhruv's father planted a Glenlivet on the rocks in Nikki's hands.

'You're always spoiling them.' Dhruv's mother hissed, popping a salted cashew nut into her mouth.

'I see my daughter once in a year, how am I spoiling her? Tell her Dhruv.'

'Dad's right, Nikki's already spoilt; she can't get any worse.' Dhruv aimed a balled-up paper napkin at his sister.

'What's all this commotion? I turn my back for a few minutes, and I miss out on all the fun.' Zasha joined her father at hurling crushed napkins at Nikki. 'Paper fight! Paper fight!' She cheered.

'It's so good to have our children at home with us.' Dhruv's dad stroked his wife's hand to get her to try and relax. 'Both the girls will be gone in a month, and then you'll cry about how far they are. Let them be.'

By half-past one, Zasha had been introduced to fourteen relatives. It was way too much for her to try and remember their names: nicknames and given names. The elders were going to be just 'aunty' and 'uncle'. Everyone called the toddler 'baby' so that was taken care of; Zasha was now left with learning the names of her cousins: Nikhil, Pia, Khushi, and Aarav (who Zasha believed should have been named itchy since he would not stop fiddling with his male jewels).

While Khushi was borderline annoying, Zasha couldn't decide if Nikhil was reserved or just pretending to have an air of mystery surrounding him. Pia, on the other hand, was a welcome surprise; she was kind and inclusive. Pia wasn't a typical ten-year-old in love with jewellery and all things Disney. While she was still into Roald Dahl, they had one common love: the Harry Potter series. When Pia learned that Zasha enjoyed charcoals she promised to take her to an art store her teacher swore by for supplies. But Zasha would have to convince Pia's mother to drive them there, as she was banned from visiting the store for two months, given that her last trip to the store cost her parents a five-figure bill.

'Beta it's been such a long time since we've seen you. You were around Khushi's age when you came down for—' Dhruv's maternal aunt observed.

'Dad's wedding. This is only my second time to India.' Zasha completed. Dhruv's folks couldn't get around the fact that Eira was comfortable with Dhruv getting married to someone else and even attended the wedding when she could have been the one sitting in the *mandap*.

'You should visit more often.' One of the uncles said. 'Or maybe we should come to see you during the Christmas holidays.'

'No.' Zasha tipped into a panic. 'I mean…I plan to visit every other year.'

Zasha knew Eira would never approve having extended family over for the holidays. Christmas and Birthdays were extra special to Eira. Any other day she might have considered hosting Dhruv's cousins and their families, even if it meant having a few members cramped up on the carpet in sleeping bags in their tiny living room. However, now that they were moving to a new house, there was a good chance they could have people staying over more often.

With some help from Nikki, Dhruv's mother succeeded at impressing Zasha with a mean Shirley Temple: the kids were thrilled about having their very own colourful mocktails, even though Khushi whined about "too much" crushed ice. Nikki convinced her mother to ditch the plastic cups and serve the kids their drinks in fancy long-stemmed glasses. Lunch was served early for the first time in the Kapur lunch history. At get-togethers, they usually ate at a respectable three-thirty or so, after having filled their bellies with all sorts of appetizers and drinks, of course.

'You know, I feel really bad for Zasha. She's such a lovely girl. I still don't understand why Eira won't marry Dhruv. He's single again; maybe they are destined to be together. Look at how her previous relationship ended.' Aarav's mom straightened her posture and looked around for approval from the other ladies.

'Eira is fighting the inevitable.' Khushi's mother agreed. 'Children are supposed to be God's gift; they bring parents closer. It's puzzling, in their case they only seem to be drifting further and further away.' She added.

'She's leading her life the way she wants. Dhruv doesn't seem to have a problem with that. Why are you'll so worried? Take a chill pill.' Pia's mother felt a small tug at her legs when she whipped around to see what it was. The baby was holding on to her dupatta. At this point, her eyes fell on Zasha who was standing two feet away, at the kitchen door. The other two heads swivelled towards Zasha in synchronized robotic movements.

'She's a good mom. You don't know her, and it's easy for everyone to assume she is crazy...'

'Sweetie, please don't be upset, you misunderstood. We were just—' Pia's mom's cheeks burned with embarrassment.

'I know people talk about us, and we don't expect other people to understand. Every family has their own circus.' Zasha placed her empty dessert bowl in the sink and left them to their conversation.

The afternoon stretched, and the party continued into the evening with everyone returning to their respective homes after masala chai and some *namkeens* and *mithai*. Zasha was semi-comatose after all the "try this", "just one bite", "oh, you'll love this one", "you're on *chutti*." The best one being "you're a growing child." And that's when Zasha refused to eat or drink any more. Twelve was no age to be stuffing your face.

Nikki escaped the food nightmare. She was unable to keep her eyes open and politely excused herself from the party. She was grateful for Dhruv's home upstairs that allowed her to get away from the quacks in the family. Her cousins' wives were all about the deep-cleanse and crystal therapy. They were sure she'd get pregnant after a couple of tries and had even slipped her a few visiting cards of some healers who'd helped their friends conceive. Her aunts didn't shy away from recommending their spiritual guru who would have some deeper understanding about her situation. Maybe there was bad energy in her home, and she needed to organize a *havan*.

'Spill...who did you dislike the most?' Dhruv asked sensing Zasha's change in mood after dessert.

'Nobody. They're all nice. Some overly nice.'

'Still, I know these lunches. There's always someone who says something they shouldn't have.'

'Tee hee. Then you know your family a little too well. But today was uneventful.'

'If things are not fine, you'll tell me, right?'

'Yes.' She blinked. 'I really want to sit and chat, Dad...' Zasha's eyes closed involuntarily. Dhruv stared at his daughter's face; she wasn't his sweet little bubba bouncing of his knees anymore. Her features were now fuller, and even though everyone said she resembled him, he saw a faint Eira slowly making an appearance. He helped her up to her room and tucked her in bed like he always did.

Clang!

The spoon holder tipped over and landed on the floor sending the forks and spoons flying in different directions. It was the wee hours of the morning, and Nikki was up making herself a grilled cheese sandwich. The apartment was eerily silent, but she was confident she hadn't woken up her brother and niece, they slept like logs.

Nikki had a long day planned. Her father encouraged her to use the trust fund money that he'd set up in her name for the surrogacy process. She had a meeting fixed with her dad's lawyer that morning, followed by lunch with her in-laws, and then a quick inspection of the apartment Sai and she had leased out.

Nikki reached for the ceramic photo frame with three bears climbing up a birch. It held three photos of Zasha: the left one was taken when she was barely a few hours old, the middle one had her blowing out candles for her third birthday, and the right one was of Dhruv and Zasha at their first solo camping trip. Zasha had gifted this frame to Dhruv as a memory of their time together. Nikki's eyes went back to the first one: Zasha's dimpled fists were curled up, and her eyes were closed. Her rosebud mouth nestled between her full pink cheeks. That's exactly what Nikki wanted. Just that. The joy of breathing in the smell of her own baby's soft head and holding her child close to her bosom while he or she entwined their little fingers with hers. Nikki wanted two: a boy and a girl, like Dhruv and her. Now that she was *this* close to having a baby, she could barely think about anything else. If all went well, she was considering cutting back on work hours so that she would have enough time to spend with her baby. Nikki was confident her business partner would understand, she'd been there too, and Nikki had been accommodating. It was her turn to enter *mommyville*. She would have her hands full with diapers, organic baby food, and play dates. Nikki was simply desperate to disappear into the cloud of motherhood.

Chapter Fourteen

'Have you come up with another name for your baby?' Dhruv massaged the muscles in Nikki's shoulders running his thumb in circular motions.

'Ouch.' Nikki flinched. 'Don't ever do that to any other woman. You pinched my skin. And don't sneak up on me like that again.'

'Your muscles are all knotted. You should get a massage; this baby making is driving you nuts. You have a permanent scowl on your face.' Dhruv screwed up his face to show her the look. 'Want some coffee?'

'Yes, for the coffee, and NO I do not look like that.'

'Ask Mummy.'

'As if she would disagree with anything that falls out of your mouth.'

'See, that's what I mean…unnecessary sarcasm.' Dhruv pulled out two coffee mugs from the cabinet and placed them on the kitchen counter.

'Maybe. It's easy for you to say. You're not struggling to have a child.'

'I've lost my wife; I have a daughter who lives thousands of miles away from me, and I live two floors above my parents' home. That last one is the only decision I thoroughly regret, and I have my dead wife to blame for that. I'd understand if she said she loved the Bandstand sea-view. It is fabulous to wake up to a rising sun, but she wanted to be close to family. She wanted to have large communal meals. I wasn't our mummy's favourite when my wife was alive. She was. I would have certainly preferred to live at least a few streets away. In fact, I would have never moved back from the US.'

'Are we seriously comparing whose life is worse?'

'You win. Fine. Your life sucks more than mine.'

'Dhruv, this is my last chance, okay. My eggs won't be viable forever. I'm banking on our surrogate being able to get pregnant the first time itself. There's too much pressure.'

'It's not life and death, Nik. You have Sai, and as far as I know him, you're all he cares about.'

'Eira says the same thing.'

'Because it is true. After a point, he won't care about the absence of a child as long as he has you, the one he promised to spend his life with. And your in-laws are such lovely people. They aren't the, "Koi good news?" kind. Pregnancy brouhaha is for our family.' Dhruv laughed.

'C'mere, you. I need a hug.'

'Can you let go of that photo frame? You're clutching it too tight. I love that frame.' Dhruv gently took it out of her hands and placed it back on the unit. His eyes wandered along the line of frames that were mounted on his wall; Eira was up on it too. His eyes locked on a honeymoon photo; his wife was his one true love, his soul mate. He'd never felt like that with anyone else before. It was magic! Maybe Eira was right all along by not forcing marriage upon themselves; he would have landed up missing out on his one big love, a love that he wanted to hold on to for the rest of his life.

Nikki gave Dhruv's advice some thought and went off for a run along the promenade. It was a quiet and peaceful morning until Salman Bhai made a brief appearance on his bicycle, and then suddenly out of nowhere a mob of fans thronged the promenade. The Khan family members were no strangers to the residents of Bandstand. Nikki continued with her run and stood outside Galaxy Apartments like a star-struck fan. It was fun watching people go crazy while waiting to catch a glimpse of their favourite film star in the hope that he'd turn around and wave out to them. Oh, the magic of Bollywood!

Zasha had slept through the night and was bright and chirpy that morning. She filled her Nani in on all the gossip from the previous day. The Cats were uncontrollable.

'Dad has the entire day planned. I have no clue where he's taking me today. He has taken three weeks off in total: the first and last week that I'm here and then one week when he's travelling back with me.' Zasha said, as she tried to pair her jeans with a suitable top.' There were four t-shirts and one sleeveless blouse strewn on her bed. 'Which one, Nani?' She raised up two hangers.

'Purple.'

'Nah, I like the yellow one better. Thanks anyway.'

Kanika shook her head in defeat. 'Hola' Eira poked her head in, 'Did you give your cousins the prezzies I sent?'

'Yup and they opened them right away. One had a price tag left on it.'

'Oh, no.'

'Mom, you did it on purpose.' She giggled.

'I did not. How cheap do you think I am?'

'Eight dollars cheap. Luckily I saw it and pulled it off the sippy cup before anyone else saw it.'

'An eight-dollar sippy cup ain't cheap missy.'

'You should see that baby? He's hideous.' Zasha's hands flew to her face in horror.

'Ha ha. You are mean.'

'Just telling it the way it is, Mom. He has this eerie smile and a weird mop of hair on his head and everyone's going goo goo gaga over him as if he's one of Prince William's babies.'

'All babies are cute. Stop being rude,' Nani interrupted.

'Mummy, hideous looking adults don't pop out of nowhere. They had to have been hideous looking when they were growing up too.' Eira chuckled.

'You two are unbelievable.' Nani adjusted her spectacles. 'Keep your voice down. You don't want Dhruv thinking you are bad mouthing his cousin's kid.'

'Dad's chilled out. I love hanging with him.' An uneasy chill went down Eira's spine. 'My room's nice and large here, and we're going to buy some stuff to decorate it, so I don't miss home too much while I'm here.'

Miss home...while I'm here. Eira's ears pricked up. Zasha wasn't contemplating living with her dad forever. Eira let out an audible sigh of relief.

⸺◌◌◌⸺

'Dad, don't you want to get into something more comfortable... shorts maybe?' Zasha gave Dhruv a quick once-over.

'Umm, this is comfy,' he said, running his hands along his new khaki chinos. You don't approve?'

'You're crushing it, Dad. You look good, as always.'

'Do you want something from me?' Dhruv suspected a wheedling tone.

'Ha ha no *no*. I was simply paying you a genuine compliment. I'm sure Mom thinks you are handsome too,' she mumbled.

'Come again?'

'Nothing, let's go.' Zasha hastily picked up her polka dotted canvas backpack and slipped on her shoes. 'First stop?'

'Pia's mother messaged me the directions to the art store you and Pia spoke about yesterday. She offered to take you there, but then I thought I should take you there myself. Good idea?'

'Brilliant.'

Zasha spent the morning in the company of canvases, Chungking bristles, polypack rolls, and charcoal graphite leads; she was spoiled for choice. The Palette was definitely an art heaven with supplies from around the world. Two hours later, they left the store with an easel stand, two bags of charcoal painting supplies, and three sealed boxes of some more art stuff, which she could take back with her.

'I couldn't have asked for a better start to my stay, Dad. Thank you so very much. I can't wait to show Mia my loot.'

'Ha ha right choice of words. That store did loot us. The last brush I picked up was a Camlin, twenty-five years ago. I nearly died when he said that hog hair bristle brush cost ₹2600.'

'Dad you sound old.' Zasha eyes widened.

'Someday you'll get there too, my girl. But for now, tell me what you'd like to eat for lunch.'

Zasha fished out a list from her bag and gave it to Dhruv to pick a restaurant that would serve any one item on the Must-Eat list. Dhruv perused her list:

- *Paani Puri*

- *Sev Puri*

- *Mishti Doi*

- *Khasta Kachori*

- *Aloo Chaat*

- *Rajasthani Thali*

'Minus the thali, this is a snack list, not lunch *lunch*.' Dhruv pointed out.

'I'm still stuffed from that delicious breakfast. I want to have something light and spicy. Don't worry, I have Mom's list that she wants me to eat on her behalf, so we have time.'

'Okay then since we're in Chowpatty itself, let's eat at Cream Centre. You can eat their famous spicy chaat, *Bambaiya Ragda*, and I will order my usual.' Dhruv suggested, as he clicked open the car boot. A few minutes later, they were seated at a table overlooking the choppy waters of the Arabian Sea. The sky now a shade of gravel grey had notoriously changed colour since they stepped out that morning. Plump drops of moisture fell to the ground making the dust from the road rise, filling the air with a distinct baked-earth smell. The first rains. Lightning split the sky followed by a loud clap of thunder. And then without a warning, a wall of rain poured down lasting all of seven minutes.

'I'm so glad we got in on time or we would have been soaking wet while walking here.'

'I love it here, Dad. Mumbai has its own charm.'

'Why do you think I never returned to the US?' Dhruv placed his palm over hers. 'Zasha, I'm going to ask you something now, and I want you to be brutally honest with me.'

Zasha's eyebrows bunched up.

'Why did you decide to visit me?'

'Because your 40th birthday is coming up, and I missed you.'

'And?'

'And I had two months of vacation.' She stalled.

'Zasha!'

'And I just needed some space.'

'From whom?'

'Mom and her new love.'

'You don't like him?'

'I don't know him to like or not like him.'

'So then?' Dhruv pressed.

'I don't want to see her hurt again, and honestly; I don't want any other man besides you in our home now. Men are all lying slugs, except for you, Dad.'

'Zasha, your mother won't let that happen again. She was in love and misjudged the man.'

'All of us had to pay for her mistake.' Zasha tilted her chin and stared at the ceiling.

'Would you feel the same way if I decided to get married again?'

'Are you?' Zasha's heart sank.

'Hypothetically speaking, sweetheart.'

'Are you thinking about it, Dad?'

'No. Never again. I lost the love of my life; I'm done. I'm happy being on my own now.'

'Why can't she be happy alone?'

'I probably shouldn't be having this conversation with you so early...but I believe you are smart enough to understand what I am going to say. Zasha, love does not politely knock on your door and ask you if you would like to allow a person in...love's more like a gatecrasher. And then once that someone is in your life, their presence is like an addiction. You don't want to let go. Shikhar was a hard phase for your mom, but she pulled out almost immediately to keep you safe. I don't know if he was the love of her life, but she did love him, and he betrayed her trust.

'You're siding with Mom?' Zasha shifted in her chair. 'This is so messed up.'

'I'm not taking sides, which is why I asked you if there was something you didn't like about this new guy.'

'His name's Dr Nihal Zane.'

'I intend to meet him the week I'm in D.C.'

'You do? What did Mom say?'

'I haven't told her yet, but I will mention it to her the next time we speak. I wanted to have this chat with you first.'

'Don't you want to be with us, Dad?' Zasha asked, feeling sorry for herself. 'Why can't we all live together as one family like normal people. Mom and you don't even know if you will hate living under the same roof. What if this is destiny? You'll are both finally single again after such a long time. Aarav's mum thinks so.'

'Zasha, I don't know why Aarav's mother needs to have an opinion about Eira and me, but I need to ask you, did you come to visit me to bring us together?' This time Dhruv was direct.

Zasha mulled over the question for a few seconds. 'No, that idea just popped in my head right now.' She claimed.

Dhruv didn't believe her for a second, but he had hoped she would be honest about it. 'Little girl, Eira and I like each other. We're not star-crossed lovers or bitter about the other's life. She will always be special to me, and I will always be there to support you'll in every way I can. You guys are my family…both before and after I got married too. But Eira and I don't love each other in a romantic sort of way.'

'I hear romance flies outta the window when people get married… see, you're in luck, you'll don't have to worry about having lost it.'

'Ha ha.' Dhruv shook his head and let out an amused laugh making the other patrons turn their heads towards them. 'Where are you getting all your love tips from?'

'The salon.'

'You read those magazines they keep in the waiting area. The ones where half the magazine is dedicated to advising women on accepting themselves the way they are, with all their flaws and then the other half is dedicated to tips on how to lose 10 pounds in a week.'

'So, you've read Nikki aunty's stash too. I flip through them, but for some reason, older women find the salon a safe haven, where they can discuss their relationships. Women usually come in pairs and are seated side-by-side discussing their loveless lives or are busy chatting on their phones so loud, as if they want the rest of the world to hear their conversations. Mia's cousin is a hairdresser at the salon, where I get my haircut. She says some women open up to her just because they want to talk, but they don't want her to give them any advice. They feel better once they've admired their perfectly styled hair. It works like magic every time.' Zasha sipped on her pink strawberry soda.

'I need to tell Eira to take you to a new salon where everyone's going about their stuff in complete silence.' Dhruv said, spreading a napkin over his chinos. 'Honey, you can't base your decisions on what's happening to others.' He turned towards the rain-lashed window remembering the time he nearly resented Eira for not marrying him. He had two friends in a situation similar to his own, and while the first friend married the woman, who was pregnant with his child, the second couple chose to live-in together. Eventually, they did get married and then divorced too in a couple of years. It had taken him some time to accept that all relationships had their own path, even if they began alike. Zasha was not even thirteen, and it was evidently confusing for her to see her parents choose other people when they were right there standing before each other refusing to give their own relationship a try.

'For now, let's put this chat on hold. We're here to enjoy this chaat and chaana masala, so let's be present in this moment. Nihal's not going away any time soon.'

'You don't say!' Zasha cocked her head, digging her fork into the mushy pattice. 'I'd like one of those after lunch.' Zasha hoicked a thumb towards the table opposite theirs where a little boy was devouring large mouthfuls of mango *kulfi*.

Chapter Fifteen

After lunch, Dhruv and Zasha strolled along the wet promenade talking about her new love for coffee, about Mia, the stress of being a gifted middle schooler, and the perks of being a brown-skinned first-generation American. Dhruv was glad to know the colour of her skin was not holding her back from achieving her goals. It was comforting to see his daughter open up to him and share little details of her life without thinking twice. Lost in conversation, they had walked right up to Kamala Nehru Park. Dhruv wanted her to get a view of the spectacular Queen's Necklace from the park's viewing deck, but the park was closed for renovation. Of course, there was always Dome, the open-air lounge and terrace restaurant with a breathtaking night view of the same area, and Nikki would be happy to join them too for old time's sake. But he was a bit disappointed that Zasha would miss seeing the iconic Old Lady's shoe at the park too, although he knew she was much older for that sort of entertainment. He simply wanted to share bits of his own childhood with her, and this park was full of those memories.

Later that evening when they got home, Nikki hadn't returned yet. She'd been sending him agitated texts all day about being stuck in mind-numbing bumper-to-bumper traffic everywhere she went. Nikki was irate with Dhruv for not warning her about the metro rail work and all the chaos that accompanied it.

'Zasha, I don't think your aunt is going to be in high spirits when she's back. Do you want to hit the pool with Pia and Nikhil? Their mother just messaged that they are going for a swim.'

'Will Khushi be there too?'

'I would think yes. Why?'

'She's irritating!' Zasha tilted her head giving him the as-if-you-didn't-know expression.

'Come on, now. She's little and wants to be part of the older kids' gang,' Dhruv said, reading the last of Nikki's swear messages she'd texted him.

'Dad, it's me, Zasha. You can tell me what you really think about her.'

'Ha ha. That is my honest opinion. But it's also true that she does get under my skin with her high pitch and whining.'

'I knew it. I knew it,' Zasha repeated, pointing her index finger towards him.

'Don't gloat about your observation. Go change into your swimsuit. They'll be up in a few minutes. It's on the fifth floor, right by the fitness centre, left from the table tennis room.'

'If you have a pool and TT room here...' Zasha smiled, thinking about her grandmother's reaction to her poor knowledge of the game, '...why does Daadi want me to go to this Bandra gym?'

'To show off her granddaughter to her school friends! She goes there once a month to play bridge with them. Papa and I haven't been to the gymkhana in years. If he's missing from his office or from home, we know now, to first check at the BPGC.'

'BPGC?'

'The Bombay Presidency Golf Club. Papa and Mummy, they love hanging out with their school buddies.'

'I hope Mia and I stay friends forever too.'

'Look at Eira and Nikki. They are as thick as thieves.'

'They are college friends.'

'Still, it takes a lot of commitment and love to stay friends all these years. I don't have any friend I've stayed in touch with from school or college.' Dhruv handed her a fresh pool towel when the doorbell rang. A bright-faced Pia dressed in a lime-green swimsuit stood at the door with Khushi by her side looking up at Zasha with saucer eyes.

'I've been waiting for you. We must hurry, the boys will hog the pool chairs with their wet stinky swimming shorts,' Pia grumbled, adjusting her Lion King printed towel around her, so it wouldn't ride down her waist.

'Relax. I'm coming.' Zasha picked up her swimming glasses and mumbled to Dhruv, 'Pia was supposed to be the sane one.'

'Have fun kids,' Dhruv patted them on their way out. 'Zasha, stay safe.'

Khushi skipped ahead of them in her noisy plastic flip-flops genuinely excited about pushing the elevator button.

'I went to The Palette today with Dad. Thank you so very much, Pia.'

'Did you like it?'

'OMG. I loved the place. It is close to impossible to stay in control in that store. I wanted to buy just about everything. Actually, I did buy a lot of stuff and one tiny thing for you too.'

'You did? Thanks, *yaar*, what is it?'

'It's a surprise. Come over later, and I'll give it to you.'

Pia was right, when they'd reached the pool area, Zasha noticed a bunch of boys sprawling themselves on four of the five loungers, while three girls huddled up on one.

'Meet my cousin, Zasha,' Pia introduced her to the girls. Zasha tried to guess their age: the girl with the thick glasses came across as a ten-year-old, and the other two were fourteen or older. They had boobs.

'Nice to meet you Zasha.' The girls chorused.

'Same here.' Her American accent spilt out of her mouth garnering the attention of the boys who had scanners for eyes. They'd given her a quick once over, and the smirk on their faces was a sign that they were fairly pleased with their assessment.

'Priyanka Chopra's in the house.' The one with the crooked yellow teeth muttered.

'That's my sister, Zasha. She was born in New York, you dufus.' Nikhil playfully swatted the cap off the boy's head.

'Sorry, bro. I love PC's accent.'

'You love much more than her accent,' Gaurav insisted. The others guffawed at his wit with relish.

'Don't mind these goons, Zasha,' Nikhil called out.

'I've seen worse.'

'Who are you guys talking to?' Ari asked, pulling out his earplugs. He ran both hands through his glossy mane that fell perfectly over his decently pleasant face. Fourteen-year-old Ari was no teenage model, what he possessed was an air of cool and casual confidence that reached his eyes when he spoke making them sparkle like lodestars lighting up his face. Ari was a star athlete at his school and was now training for the state-level tennis championship. Nikhil and Ari were best friends and did nearly everything together.

'Nikhil's cousin is visiting. We were just taking her case,' Gaurav replied.

'Really? And how may I ask?' Zasha was now standing right behind him with hands folded against her chest.

'Sorry. Gaurav's just being silly.' Ari apologized; his ebony black eyes locked with hers.

'Says the charmer.' Gaurav mumbled loud enough for Zasha's ears and walked over to join the girls at their swim race. The other two boys followed behind.

'Have you moved to this building?' Ari continued.

'No, just visiting.'

'Oh, and how long do you plan to stay?'

'A month. It's my third day here.' Zasha realized she was giving more information than she was being asked.

'This is my last year of freedom. After that, I'm going to have to slog my ass off for the next three years…must get into a good college. I want to go to London and study when I graduate from high school, but my parents have other plans. I'm going to run away.'

'What!' Zasha's eyes nearly popped out. 'I'm not party to this conversation. Please don't say anything further.'

'Ha ha I was kidding. I'm not stupid. What about you, which grade?'

'I don't plan to run away. So, I'll continue at the same school for the next five years.'

'Cheeky girl,' Ari winked.

'Nikhil and the gang…do you guys attend the same school?'

'Yup. We don't get enough of each other at school, so we hang out at home too.' Ari continued in his jocose disposition.

'Ari,' Nikhil called out, cutting into their conversation. 'What are you doing? Come on, jump in with us.'

'In a bit.' Ari replied, twisting the orange macramé bracelet around his wrist.

'We need you, bro. The girls are up by one point.' Gaurav yelled. There was an awkward moment of silence between them when

Zasha got up and walked towards the pool to join the others, and Ari quickly followed behind.

In the end, the boys beat the girls by three laps, and they were going to celebrate with some ice-cream after they dried off. Pia and Khushi had a 7 p.m. curfew, and so they left. The other girls were joining Ari and the boys.

'Nikhil why don't you invite Zasha to come with us? It's our duty to be nice to your guest,' Ari reasoned.

'I don't think she will. Pia's gone home,' Nihal replied grudgingly.

'Are you her mouthpiece?' Gaurav teased.

'Whatever. Zasha do you want to join us for ice cream?' Nikhil asked half-heartedly.

'You can't say no to 236 flavours,' Ari made his case.

Zasha sensed Nikhil's discomfort; there was something odd about his behaviour. 'I'm still jet-lagged. I'm gonna head home.' She cobbled together, masking her disappointment.

'Here, keep this and tell me what you think tomorrow.' Ari shoved his iPod touch in her hand. Zasha's face was on fire; she knew there were six pairs of eyes pinned on her waiting for her to make her next move. It was indeed the beginning of a budding friendship.

'What kind of music's on it?' She managed to ask.

'The kind you love or will fall in love with, I promise. See you tomorrow.'

Ari threw his hands around Nikhil and Gaurav and herded them towards the gates. He had made sure he would see her again the next day. Zasha hurried upstairs clutching the iPod to her chest unable to wipe off the smile on her face. When she rang the doorbell, there was no answer. She ran downstairs to her grandparents' home and just as she had expected, Dhruv was having a cup of tea with his parents. Nikki was home too and in an uncommonly chirpy mood despite her earlier misadventures with Mumbai traffic.

'Come, come.' Nikki held her hand out to Zasha. 'I have some great news.'

'Tell us already. We're all here now,' Dhruv persisted.

'Sai called earlier, and he said we'd made it to Step 2. The agency has found a potential match, and they've done the preliminary background checks. We are now awaiting her medical and psychological screenings results.' Nikki shared, delirious with relief.

'*Bhadaiyaan, beta*. It's all God's grace. *Tum dekho*, going forward, everything will fall in order.' Her mother swaddled her in a warm, protective hug. 'We must go to *Siddhi Vinayak* next week and offer thanks to God.' Nikki agreed immediately to her mother's surprise.

'This is super-hot news Nikki aunty. Mom will be so pleased when I tell her…unless you've already told her.' Zasha snuggled up to her aunt. 'Soon I'll have a little cousin to fuss over. I've always wanted siblings; God's finally answering my prayers.'

'Slow down girl. We have a long way to go.' Nikki said, curling her legs up on the couch-style diwan. 'Dhruv, what's the name of that tree house place we're going to for your birthday?' Nikki didn't want to talk about the future in great detail. This baby was far too important for her to allow anything to jinx it.

'The Machan in Lonavala.'

'I *hope* they have cell phone network there. I don't want to miss any updates from Sai.'

'I'm not sure. Give him the resort landline number. If he can't reach any of us, ask him to call the resort and leave a message for you.'

'That means you aren't expecting them to have good network.'

'I don't know. I haven't been there before; some colleagues at work recommended the place.'

'*Fiine*, I'll figure a way to stay in touch with Sai.' Nikki bit into an *ajwa khajur* (her favourite kind from the Bateel boutique store in

Dubai) that her mother passed around, to celebrate the *muh-meetha* moment.

'What's with the Julia Robert smile?' Nikki was surprised to see Zasha so jubilant. Her perpetually frowning face had a wide grin plastered on it. Nikki was certain it had little to do with the news she'd just shared. Her eyes shifted to the iPod in Zasha's hand.

'Dhruv bought you that?' She asked, pointing towards it. 'No wonder you're so cheerful.'

'No, that's not mine. Nikhil's friend allowed me to borrow it for a night.'

'I'm glad Nikhil's being inclusive and not his usual possessive self,' Dhruv observed.

'Yea he's not at all possessive,' Zasha agreed.

They didn't have to know Nikhil had been a jerk to her. Besides, she didn't want to jeopardize meeting Ari the next day. If Nikhil got into trouble, there was a slim chance his friends would hang out with her again.

Chapter Sixteen

Twelve Hours Earlier

D.C., U.S.A

'Come over tonight,' Nihal said, his voice half pleading, while continuing to examine the post-op and pre-op X-rays mounted on the view box. Unfortunately, there was very little difference between the two reports. His four-year-old patient, who had already undergone three surgeries that year, was slowly running out of options.

'Don't get too comfortable with me coming over to your place. Zasha will be back in less than a month.' Eira was glad to be counting down the days until her daughter returned.

'It's only 7.30 p.m. I had a shitty day, we can—'

'So, this is a booty call.'

'Arrgh. I was going to say, have dinner, and talk, and maybe booty up a little too.'

'Not tonight. I'm in my PJs and in bed with Sophie Kinsella.'

'Oooh, are we having phone sex.'

'Sophie's a New York Times bestselling author you idiot.'

'I knew that.'

'No, you didn't. You have a dirty mind.'

'You bring out the dirty in me,' Nihal said, shutting his office door behind him. The interns had their ears cocked up for hot gossip. 'Babe, I was wondering…if you're free this weekend. I'm going to meet my folks, and I would like you to join me. Peaks of Otter is approximately a four-hour drive from here, and with Zasha in India I think the timing is perfect.'

'This weekend's like four days away.'

'Do you have someplace else to be?'

'No. I…' Eira bit into her cuticles. 'I have to prepare my mind first before I meet your parents, besides, Zasha might flip out if she knows I went to see them.'

'Did you make her any false promises about breaking up with me?'

'Not at all, but the timing doesn't seem right.'

'A month ago, I know you said you had to think about it, but then, Zasha had no plans of going to India, and you would have probably had to force her to go with you. Now you don't.'

'That's true.'

'So then?'

'I don't know…' a shiver went down her spine '… these are your parents and—'

'I ain't throwing you to the wolves; besides, I'll be there with you 24/7. This could be our first vacation of sorts. And Kanika is always there to play buffer.'

'Oh, my mother is invited too?'

'Of course. I'm sure she would want to meet the parents of her daughter's boyfriend.'

'Can you stop using that word?'

'Which one?'

'Boyyyfrriend.'

'What do you refer to me as?'

'Umm. Nihal.'

'Yes. But if you were to formally introduce me to someone, *Meet Nihal, myyy…*'

'Nihal—'

'We're going to be meeting family and friends soon. We have three weeks to ourselves, and I want the guys to meet my not-so-imaginary-girlfriend.'

'Give me a day to think about it, as for tonight I'm staying in.' Eira tried to swerve back into their earlier conversation.

'My parents will love you. I came to your home knowing well it was a minefield, and I survived. I'm ready to take the next step and introduce you to my parents. I'm in this for real.'

'I will give it a good thought, Nihal. I just need to sleep on it. I have to make sure Zasha is fully in the loop. She still hasn't spoken to me about you after that introductory dinner, and then she took off to India. I'm struggling to understand what's going on in her mind. I am extremely insecure right now, and I've never felt like this before. I want her to spend time with Dhruv, but you know she didn't decide to go to India just because she wanted to hang out with him. Anything can set her off, and I don't want her thinking that living with her father is a better option.' Eira choked a little. 'I can't live without my baby girl.'

'Please don't cry. Honey, don't cry. I don't want you to feel pressurized. You sleep on it; I'm cool with whatever you decide…I love you.'

'I promise I will think about it and do my best to make this weekend happen.'

'Cheer up. I know you will do what's best for all of us.' Nihal blew her a kiss through the phone. 'Also, I think you should know that my little brother's going to be there too. Please don't let that affect your decision. He's a great guy…just very different from me.'

'How different?'

'You'll see for yourself.'

'I haven't said yes yet.'

'I know, that's me being optimistic.' Nihal's pager went off. 'Got to go, a patient needs me. Talk soon.'

Eira paged through her organizer. The cleaners weren't booked, and there were no dental appointments scheduled for that weekend. No prior social commitments either. Her weekend was as clear as a mid-summer night sky. Eira googled The Peaks of Otter on her phone. She was convinced her mother would love the place going by the images that popped up on her screen: neo-tropical animals, migratory passerines, and mountain and lake views. But it was the Sharp Top trail that caught her attention. Nihal and she both loved the outdoors, and this would give them a good chance to try out different stuff together.

Ping!

Eira's phone lit up.

Nihal: *Check this out <u>www.virginiapeaks.com</u>*

She clicked on the link; it opened to a page with photos of apple orchards. Kanika would love it. The fifteen-room lodge overlooking the orchards looked clean and cosy. *If we're staying with his parents why is he sending me these links*, Eira wondered, and then she moved the cursor and clicked on About Us. There they were, his parents, the proud, smiling owners of this picturesque getaway. Eira knew his dad had retired from medicine and that his mother was only too happy to move as far away as possible from the John Hopkins Hospital neighbourhood, but he'd left out the bit that they weren't just average pensioners, they were bloody wealthy owners of orchards and a 4-star-rated lodge. Clearly, Nihal enjoyed keeping a low profile. His parents appeared much younger in the photos on the website in sharp contrast with the ones in his living room. The website photos were probably taken a few years ago, because his mother still had her hair dyed copper-brown in them.

The sound of canned laughter seeped through her door. Kanika was tuned into The Big Bang Theory and was enjoying a good laugh.

'Mummy,' Eira padded down the stairs. 'Are these re-runs?'

'Yes,' Kanika replied, pausing the American sitcom.

'Nihal called earlier. Do you remember when he was here for dinner, he'd suggested a trip to Peaks of Otter.'

'I do,' Kanika nodded a knowing smile, confident about what was going to come next.

'Nihal's going to see his family this weekend, and he wants us to join him.'

'Us?'

'You too. Are you cool with that?'

'If you are, I am.'

'I haven't made up my mind yet. I just wanted to know if you were ok with going.'

'Is Zasha holding you back?'

'Of course.'

'She doesn't need to know.'

'I'm not going to lie to her.'

'I didn't ask you to lie, just hold on to the truth until she is back.'

'It's just too weird. Last weekend too, I didn't tell her I met Nihal.'

'You don't need to give a child a run-down of your schedule or the people you meet. Eira, I know you've tried to treat her like an adult and are more like friends, but you are the parent here, and you will have to make some decisions on your own.'

'You're cool spending a weekend with his family, right?'

'Is this a trick question?'

'Got it. Thanks, Mummy.' Eira smiled. The grudge she had held so passionately for nearly two decades was gradually yet steadily slipping away, allowing her to open her heart and make room for love for her mother once again.

∽᧚∾

Ping! Ping! Ping! Eira's phone beeped continuously.

Photo 1: My new babies (these brushes are divine, Mom).

Photo 2: Chaat @ Cream Centre

Photo 3: Guess what!

In a matter of seconds, Zasha's phone was ringing.

'Hi, so you conned your father into buying you the iPod?' Eira had been concerned Dhruv would indulge his daughter just as he did when he visited them. But she always kept a close eye and made Zasha return stuff she didn't need and buy more age-appropriate stuff using the credit coupons. How was she supposed to do that with them miles away now?

'What are you talking about?'

'Photo 3?'

Zasha was in a state of shock. Photo 3 was meant for Mia's eyes only. In a hurry, she'd probably confused the two chat windows.

'Mom, that's not mine.' Zasha straightened her spine trying to keep her voice stable. 'It's Nikhil's...I mean his friend's. I just borrowed it for a night to listen to his playlist.'

Eira let out an audible sigh.

'And here I was, ready to send Dhruv a stern message. Your

photos tell me you're having a good time.'

'Better than I thought. I wish you guys were here too.'

'Wow. That's a first in four days. I love you, cupcake.'

'Did Dad tell you we're going to this luxury tree house resort called Machan not too far from Mumbai? This is the only weekend Nikki aunty is here, so he planned this trip. Daada-daadi will be coming along too.'

'Nani and I were thinking about taking a short break from the city too. We may do something this weekend, haven't booked anything yet.'

'Without me?'

'You have cheek. Weren't you the one who ditched Yellowstone for Machan and left me high and dry?'

'Fine. Don't go anywhere too nice. You never go to the same place twice, so if it's a super nice place I don't want to miss out. What are your options?'

'We're thinking about going to the mountains.'

'Mom.'

Eira's heart drummed a fast beat. *Please don't ask. Please don't ask about Nihal.*

'Are you still mad at me for spending the summer with Dad?'

'No baby girl.' Tears pricked her eyes. 'Don't think about that. You'll be back here with me before you know.'

'And you'll be bugging me all over again.' Zasha broke into a giggle.

Eira was pleased to hear laughter return to their conversations, and so, she decided against telling Zasha about Nihal's invitation. The truth wasn't running away; it could wait three more weeks.

Nihal was over the moon when Eira confirmed they would be joining him on the road trip. Over the course of three days, Eira spent her lunch break shopping for new clothes. She had to get it right the first time. With Gina out of the office, Eira took longer lunch breaks and got her legs waxed, and eyebrows plucked too. Alice gave her a few tips on mountain people, despite Eira mentioning to her that Nihal's parents had only recently moved away. There was no arguing with Alice, she was completely invested in Eira's love life and had made it her pet project. Nihal wasn't helpful with gift ideas for his parents, and so, after rewinding the few conversations that they'd had about his parents in her head, she remembered they were tea lovers. Eira bought them a dainty, cobalt blue and gold porcelain tea set from *Solstice* (Alice's recommendation) and landed up burning a hole in her pocket.

Chapter Seventeen

'Damn, you're not here tomorrow. We were planning to watch a movie on the big screen. Nikhil, Gaurav…the gang.' Ari said, sounding crushed. He had disappointment scribbled all over his face.

'Which one?'

'Tube light.'

'That's the name?'

'It's a Khan movie. You watch Bollywood films, don't you?' Ari playfully bumped Zasha's shoulders.

'Sure.' Zasha wasn't going to miss the opportunity of sitting next to him in a movie hall just because she needed subtitles to understand a Bollywood movie. 'I'm back Monday morning. We can do another one next week. I mean all of us together.'

'Give me your number.' Ari handed her his phone to punch in the digits. 'If that's cool?'

From the corner of her eye, Zasha saw Nikhil watching her every move like a hawk and even though she had a gut feeling it would get her in trouble, she saved her number on his phone. Zasha had barely entered her Dad's apartment, and her phone bleeped.

Hey, save my number. Ari. ☺

Their texting marathon went on for more than an hour until Dhruv knocked for the third time reminding her that dinner had been laid on the table. Dhruv noticed a visible change in his daughter; there was a bounce in her step and a pleasant glow on her face. Zasha did not bring up her mother's love life again, and Eira wasn't messaging him about any strange attitude from Zasha. He liked to believe that he had some part to play in the positive change.

01 July 2017

Washington, D.C., USA

Eira threw in one last pair of shorts into her suitcase and let it thud shut. It was a little after 6 a.m., and the sun was blooming in the sky like an orange marigold. Eira heard the crunch of the tyres of Nihal's mid-size SUV announcing his arrival. She surveyed her bedroom one last time; everything was in its designated space. Eira hated coming home from a vacation to an unkept house. Minutes earlier, Zasha had called to tell her all about the eco-friendly tree house they'd checked into, and her visit to the Korigad fort where she had walked along the fort walls. Nikki had treated her, to her first actual street food; there was very little that could go wrong with roasted corn on the cob sprinkled with chilli powder and rubbed in with a little lime. Zasha was wrapped up in detailing her own little adventure, and before she could ask about her mother's weekend plans, Nikki hollered for help with setting up the birthday cake. Eira had been spared the awkward moment of having to cover up her tracks.

'Are we ready to leave?' Nihal snuck up behind her. He gathered her hair at the nape and landed a kiss on her neck.

'Hell ya.' Eira could barely contain her exuberance. She had butterflies in her stomach; the wheels of this trip were turning for real. 'Let's do this.'

The trio left before breakfast to avoid the 4th of July weekend rush. Like most people, Eira had taken the Monday off too, to make it a four-day weekend. The drive was turning out to be longer than expected. The traffic on the I-66 was maddening, with five lanes of cars moving forward at snail speed, thankfully a space began to open by the time they merged on to the I-81.

'We need to fuel up.'

'The tank's full.' Nihal pointed to the fuel gauge.

'I'm hungry. I haven't had my morning coffee yet.' Eira groaned. 'My tummy's growling.'

'It was you? I thought it was Yolo moaning at the back. He hates long drives when it's more people than just him and me.'

'Here. Have some of this.' Kanika offered them a box of ham and cheese sandwiches she had packed.

'You're a lifesaver, Mummy.' Eira's hand dove in and pulled out two triangles. 'Let's stop at a Starbucks and pick up some coffee to go.'

'Are your parents going to roll out the red carpet for us?' Eira broke off a piece of the sandwich and put it in Nihal's mouth.

'They reserve that for Day 2…if their guests behave well, they get the royal treatment.'

'I guess I'll keep the gift for Day 2 then.' Eira played along.

'Seriously babe, you shouldn't have bought anything. They aren't formal about these things.'

'Oh, we couldn't meet them empty-handed.' Kanika said, once again offering them the box of sandwiches. 'We're their house guests. It would be rude not to take anything.'

'How thoughtful, I guess men don't really think about all these things.'

'You bought us beautiful flowers.' Kanika reminded him about his first visit to their home.

'Or did you get one of your many interns to run off to the florist?' Eira narrowed her eyes.

'Don't give me that look. You know that isn't true. Kanika, don't listen to anything your daughter tells you about me.'

'Are you sure about that? I've only heard her say wonderful things about you.'

'Oh, so mother and daughter have ganged up against me.' Nihal peered into the rear-view mirror and caught Kanika suppressing a lark. 'It will soon be 4:2.'

Kanika dozed off for an hour, and Eira got busy texting with Nikki whose initial excitement about the potential surrogate had now changed to nervous anticipation. She couldn't help worrying about the potential surrogate's medical results – they were told their case manager would let them know in a week. None of it was in her control. *Learning to let go,* was the biggest lesson she was learning on this journey to motherhood. The surrogacy agency had given them a few books to mentally prepare them for the surrogacy process—a guide of sorts. Of course, books had been no help in the past—not during the baby-making period, nor during the healing phase. Eira reminded her that this time, she had to be stronger, not just for herself and Sai, but for the surrogate too. Nikki was a little nervous about the first meeting, it was bound to be overwhelming to meet the woman who would carry *their* child in her womb. Bizarre thoughts about the surrogate rejecting her began to cloud her mind. Eira knew that no matter what she said Nikki would not feel any better until she heard positive news from the agency. So instead, she decided to tell her about her impromptu trip to meet the Zanes, and as expected Nikki's smile returned. She too agreed that it was better to wait until Zasha returned home to tell her about their weekend. Twenty minutes into the texting and Nihal refused to drive any further if Eira kept chatting with her friend leaving him to drive in silence. Eira secretly liked that he wanted her for himself and wasn't shy about showing it in front of others.

As Nihal drove the last stretch of the trip, exiting the Blue Ridge Parkway motorway at Milepost 86, Eira drank in the pretty sights of the Appalachian mountain range, and then a few miles further, the man-made Abott Lake came into view. They were now 6 miles away, and Eira felt a knot form in the pit of her belly.

As they approached the driveway, the stone walls of the quiet country home glowed in the mid-morning sun. His parents weren't waiting for them at the doorstep, as she had expected them to be with arms wide open. Nihal parked his car behind a black two-door Jeep Cherokee. The second Nihal removed the key from the ignition the rambunctious canine had a new lease of life. Hearing Yolo bark like a prisoner released before his time, Nihal's mother, Suma, came out on the front porch. He jumped up to lick her face and then made himself comfortable on one of the two Adirondack chairs, saliva dripping from his mouth on to the seat cushion.

'Hello there, you're just in time for a second round of morning delights.' Suma greeted her son and hugged him close. 'And this must be your special lady friend.' Suma smiled opening her arms once again, this time to embrace Eira.

'Hi, Suma. It is lovely to meet you, and this is my mother, Kanika.' Eira introduced her mother. Suma didn't initiate a third hug. This time she went for a simple handshake.

'Come, come. Make yourselves comfortable. Chris will be here soon after he's done frosting the last batch of cupcakes.'

'Dad's into baking now?'

'Your father's trying his hand at everything these days, although with little success. However, baking is one thing he's been outdoing himself at, you'll see.'

'Where's the little rascal,' Nihal asked, as he let Yolo out in the garden area.

'Your brother should take another hour to get here.' Suma shrugged. 'You know his timing.'

'This is a little something for you.' Eira placed the neatly wrapped gift box in Suma's hand.

'Thank you.' Suma smiled openly appraising the gift wrapping; she had a separate conversation going on in the upper chamber. Eira could not decipher the conclusion she had reached.

'Let me give you'll a tour of the place.' Suma led Eira by the hand through the living room, and Kanika followed. The opulent interiors had an old-world charm to it; in the hallway leading to the dining room, Eira passed a table clustered with photo frames. There was one of Nihal receiving his Doctorate in medicine, a shot of Suma and Chris dressed in warm winter clothing with the Daal lake as the backdrop, and one of Alex, Nihal's younger brother, playing the piano. Behind these frames was a smaller frame holding a family vacation picture in Hawaii. It was a more recent photo compared to the others, and it was cropped to delete something or someone.

'This is our reading nook.' Suma pointed as they entered the brightness of a Kelly green-painted room with wall-to-wall bookshelves.

Kanika settled herself in a leather and caned Mahogany armchair and flipped through a paperback that lay on the coffee table overflowing with medical journals, magazines, and newspapers. The Regency style armchair was a stunning piece of décor, but it wasn't as comfortable as the much cheaper recliner in her bedroom, she concluded.

'This is a breathtaking home, Suma. You have impeccable taste in home décor,' Eira gushed.

'Thank you, but I can't take credit for this, as the first home-owners did an incredible job with this place. They had it redecorated before putting it up for sale, and we bought it as-is with the furniture. We didn't have much to bring from our old home: linen, dishes, books, clothes. What we did have were several good memories that we hold close to our heart, even today. Nihal and Alex had moved out years ago and with us spending most of our time at the hospital we had a very minimalistic home. I find this too large for the two of us, but Chris loves it here.'

'And I love it too, Mom. It's such a terrific place to just unwind.'

'Then come to visit us more often, minus your dog. He ruins my plants…look at him.' Suma pointed out to Yolo through the window.

'Now I have company on the drive here, so you'll be seeing more of us.' Nihal had used the first "us" in a sentence, and it didn't feel like a force fit. They were going public. 'I think we should check on Dad. Does he even know we're here?'

'I'm sure he heard Yolo, but once he has his hand in the batter, I've lost him.'

'Mummy, doesn't Chris remind you of Dad and his love for cooking? Oh, how he hated cleaning up after himself.' Eira reminisced. 'Strangely, those are my best memories of our time together, me sitting cross-legged on the granite kitchen platform alongside him and rolling out dough with my kiddy rolling pin.'

'Now you can roll out dough with me.' Nihal gave her nose a little tweak and wrapped his arm around her waist. 'Let's go see what my father's up to.' As they made their way towards the kitchen, a heavenly smell of freshly brewed *elaichi* chai floated through the hallway.

'Dad, these look delicious.' Nihal exchanged a man hug with his father and plopped a cupcake in his mouth licking the frosting off first.

'Any good?' Chris asked with hopeful eyes.

'Perfect to the T.'

'Good. Here, have some.' Chris offered Eira and Kanika a cupcake each. 'Welcome to our home, ladies,' he said, taking off his oven mitts to pour himself a cup of tea. 'Let's take this out to the garden since the weather is lovely for a sit out.'

'Nihal, you'll find fresh lemonade in the fridge, and coffee in the pot too. Don't be a guest.' Suma reminded him, as she helped Chris carry the trays of food outdoors.

'Yes Nihal, don't be a guest and pour me some lemonade,' Eira grinned.

'Young lady, you are no guest here either. If I'm right, we're soon going to be family,' Chris said, making a sudden re-entry into the kitchen.

He wiped his hands on a paper towel and disappeared once again through the back door before Eira could respond. Flagstone stepping-stones led the way from the kitchen's back door to the Parc yellow folding bistro table set up on the crushed stone patio. Sunlight streamed through the branches of trees that formed a canopy above them.

'So Kanika how is retired life treating you?' Chris asked.

'Better than I had expected.' Kanika replied, cutting into a loaf of banana bread. 'I keep myself busy with various projects at the women's welfare centre and the Green Feet movement. And of course, living with a tween for the second time has its own charm.'

'We can't wait to meet Zasha. I hear she's a very bright child.' Suma's eyes moved towards Eira. 'It's a shame she's not here today.'

'She sends her love.' Nihal's half-smile caught Eira's eye, and she gave him a knowing look and pursed her lips to suppress a grin.

'So, are we saving the *real conversation* for when your brother arrives or are you going to tell us already?' Suma wiped her mouth impatiently with a paper napkin.

'We waited forty years; a few minutes won't kill you.' Chris deadpanned.

Eira searched Nihal's eyes for a hint, but he was clueless. He had no idea what his parents were mumbling about.

'Oh, Nihal, don't play dumb with your old man. It's taken you nine years to get a special friend home, so you have our attention.'

Was this special friend the woman who had been poorly cropped from the photo? Eira's mind flew back to the family holiday photo frame she had seen earlier.

'We're not getting married.' Eira blurted, only seconds later wishing she could take back those words. 'I mean, we—'

'Haven't discussed marriage yet.' Nihal took over. 'I wanted our families to get to know each other first.' He said, tugging on his ear. Nihal had planned to propose to Eira on Sharp Top Mountain with the view of the lake as a backdrop, but going by Eira's response his confidence plummeted rapidly.

'Don't keep us waiting for too long. We're getting old.' Suma looked towards Kanika for a show of support.

'I agree.' Kanika slid a stray strand of hair nervously around her ear praying she'd chosen her words correctly.

Chapter Eighteen

After tea and a few more uncoordinated answers, Suma ushered her guests to their bedroom. The minute Suma left the room, Eira threw herself on the four-poster bed and breathed with ease.

'I like Nihal's parents. They are warm people with undeniably no airs about their wealth. What's your first impression of them?'

Eira nodded silently, breathing in the heady smell of freshly done laundry mixed with the sweet fragrance of peach blossom from the 3-wick jar candle Suma lit before leaving their room. Her love for candles was for everyone to see: votives in the bathrooms, flameless candles on the patio, taper candles in the dining room. *Instead of the tea set, maybe I should have gifted her candles from Pottery Barn*, Eira thought.

'Mummy, I have a gut feeling something's going to go wrong.' Eira pulled the sheets over her legs and tucked her arms inside them.

'Why? Everything has gone well so far. What's worrying you?'

'That's what's worrying. It is close to perfect, and hence unbelievable. My relationships have never been smooth sailing. There has to be some drama.' Eira contemplated, following the slow movement of the Barnwood blades of the ceiling fan rotating above her.

'Please let things flow as they are and stop overanalysing

the situation. If something crazy has to happen, it won't ask your permission before it happens. Nihal is a keeper, don't ruin it because of one lousy mistake.'

'Eira, may I come in.' Nihal knocked on the door. He had a pile of multiple sized white towels resting on his arms.

'Mom forgot these,' he said and placed them carefully on the table.

'You look pale.' He felt Eira's forehead with the back of his hand.

'I'm going to have a look at the books in your library and see if there's something I like.' Kanika excused herself and left them to talk in private.

Eira sat up in bed and reached out for his hand. 'If it's the wedding talks that's unnerving you, don't worry, they won't ask again. My parents got the message. You've frightened them.'

'What message?'

'That you're a potential Runaway Bride.'

'Shut up.' Eira threw a pillow at him, and he pulled her closer, his weight pinning her down under him.

'Wanna get frisky?'

'Have you lost your marbles? We are surrounded by our parents, and I'm sharing the room with my mother, which is why you should get off me right now.'

Nihal heard footsteps in the hallway and rolled aside immediately.

'I'm your next-door neighbour, in case you get lonely,' he simpered.

'About the last girl you "took home" nine years ago,' Eira gestured, 'are you still in touch with her?'

'Heh heh. Is that's what driving you nuts? I like that you're feeling possessive about me. Honey, I haven't seen her since we broke up. My parents still meet her parents at social gatherings, they were colleagues, but she's moved to London, and as far as I know, she's married too.'

'So, if we were to break up, your parents would cut my head out from a photo too.'

'One, that photo in the hallway is not hers. The cropped head is my brother's ex-girlfriend. My mother loves that family photo, and Alex insisted that if she wanted to put it up, it had to be minus his ex. And two, as for us breaking up, that's not going to happen.'

'What makes you so sure?'

'We'll get through whatever's thrown at us, this much I'm sure of, and that's enough for me.'

'I love that you trust in us.'

'We're good together, Eira. Don't overthink it. Now let's go downstairs, we don't want my folks thinking we're *at it*, when you're clearly opposed to the idea.'

When they came downstairs, Suma and Kanika were in the living room discussing the state of Indian politics. While Suma did not support the beef ban or the demonetization, she was all in favour of the Modi government. Every time Kanika mentioned the Congress Party, her face scrunched up. By lunchtime, the women had realized they had two common family friends back in India, although Suma had lost touch with them several years ago.

'Alex is here.' Nihal confirmed when they got back from their tour of the apple orchards. He noticed a powder blue 1957 Lincoln Premiere convertible sitting pretty in his parking spot, and it could not belong to anyone else but his brother.

'Good to see you, big brother.' Alex bumped Nihal's fist followed by a half pat on the back.

'Where is she?' Alex glanced around the room and his eyes fell on Kanika. 'There you are...' he pretended to study her, '...my brother's beautiful girlfriend.' He crossed the room to give her his signature squeeze.

'I'm the girlfriend's mother.' Kanika returned the hug with equal enthusiasm.

'Really? You're the mother of the bride-to-be? No way.'

'This one's mine.' Nihal got Alex in a headlock and pointed his index finger down at Eira.

'Now I see what he's been gushing about. Welcome to the family, Eira.' Alex kissed her on the cheek.

'Spare us the crazy talk. What took you so long to get here?' Chris asked.

'The truth: I woke up late. I'm here now, so what did I miss?'

'You've always been tardy.' Suma nodded apologetically. 'I'm glad you didn't get into medicine.'

'Nihal, let me assure you that I will get to the wedding on time and yes, I will be honoured to be your best man, but I'd still like to see a picture of the bridesmaid before I commit.'

'And this is my brother, Alex, who can't and won't stop being the funny man.' Nihal gave his brother a playful nudge.

'I'm starving.' Suma said, leading Alex and the rest to the dining room for lunch. 'Chris has worked hard on this lunch, and I tossed the Feta salad. Think of it as an early Thanksgiving meal.'

Alex continued to delight everyone with his hilarious, over-the-top stories about the American music industry. Before dinner, he played them two songs he was working on, and it was easy to see why Nihal said his brother and he were like chalk and cheese. Where Nihal was disciplined, Alex was a go-with-the flow-guy. Nihal loved baseball and Alex basketball, and while Nihal wanted to get married and have a family, Alex was content with simply enjoying the initial thrill of a relationship. If it got too serious, he bailed out. But they both had magic in their fingers. Nihal was brilliant with the scalpel and his brother with several musical instruments.

'Good morning, lovebirds.' Alex dressed in his boxer shorts and a denim jacket thrown over an old, faded t-shirt, crunched the last piece of buttered toast in his mouth.

'Put on some pants or get out of my kitchen.' Chris ordered. 'Don't sit around like a Neanderthal; we have house guests.'

'Chill Dad. You have one son dressed up as…what's that Indian comic character Mom loves? He was a detective or a hunter I can't remember…Shaamu, I think.'

'Shikari Shambu.' Eira almost spat out the fried egg.

'Oh, shut up. Just because you like the grunge look, not everyone else has to dress up like you. You are too old for that little denim jacket look you have going on there.' Nihal said, pointing his butter knife at Alex's clothes.

'Ouch. That was nasty.'

'Screw you, jackass.'

'No but seriously, it's just a hike.' Alex continued to wind up his brother, and Nihal fell for it as he did every other time.

'Shorts and a t-shirt are hiking clothes. You would know if you went on one.' It was true, Nihal had put on one of his best t-shirts, but that was because he was going to propose to Eira, and he didn't want her remembering that special moment with him down on one knee wearing his usual blue or grey t-shirts.

'Eira, don't let my brother dress your kids, especially if you have a boy.' Alex continued, eyes crinkling in his tanned face.

'You can dress yours up as little goons,' Nihal said, continuing to butter a bagel.

'Nihal won't have to worry about dressing up our kids, cause this shop is shut.' Eira rotated her finger around her belly. The room fell silent, and all eyes were now on her. Alex let her comment pass and got back to the conversation by picking on Nihal's choice of automobiles next. Eira felt Suma's gaze on her a long while after that last sentence had innocently fallen out of her mouth. She stared at her plate praying that Suma would look away soon.

Nihal parked his car near the nature centre from where they would begin the three-mile trail. The initial climb up the trail was gentle on the knees, and as they continued their hike up they exchanged hellos with several other hikers who'd had an early start to their morning and had climbed up to the summit to watch the sunrise. After two miles, Nihal stopped abruptly and sat down on one of the boulders.

'I know this isn't the right place to discuss important topics like marriage and children, but it is certainly the right time to ask you if you meant what you said earlier. Are you done with just one child?'

'Yes,' she murmured, and her eyes rested on his feet.

Nihal's face fell. For a few moments he stood silently looking far out, and then he got up and began walking back, down the trail. Eira followed him without a word.

'Eira, let me ask you this again, just so that I know I've understood you correctly.' Nihal said throwing his backpack in the back seat of his car.

'Nihal, I had Zasha at twenty-two, and while I did have my mother to support me, I've still been a single mother.'

'Phew! Enough of this single mother talk.' Nihal's voice was now an octave higher. 'We're not talking about the past. Last night before I went off to bed, I was thinking about how we could come here when we grow old and sit by the fireplace helping each other solve the crossword, while waiting for our grandkids to visit us. I want to know what you see for us in the future. In fact, do you even see us together because yesterday you were thrown off with all the wedding chatter, and today you're closed to the idea of children? Is this some way of telling me that you're not interested in a long-term relationship because I bloody hell came here today to give you this?' Nihal pulled out the box from his pocket and flipped it open. A hand-fabricated, vintage ring with a 3.14ct cushion cut sapphire sat primly in a soft velvet box and stared at her with accusing eyes.

'It's been in our family for three generations. Last night, my mother sat me down to talk about your wedding fears, and I told her that I hadn't proposed to you yet, which is when she gave me this. I bought you a diamond ring, but she insisted that I give you this one, since it's always given to the elder son's wife in the family. Now you tell me, are we considering a future together or not? Cause in my future, I see Zasha and another baby too.'

'This is more like an ultimatum.' Eira finally spoke up.

'Call it what you may.'

'Nihal, I'm in my mid-thirties. I don't have the energy to bring up another child.'

'You don't have to do it on your own this time. I will be there with you, for Christ's sake.'

'What if you land up firing blanks, and we can't have kids?'

'In that case, you get what you want. I won't feel emasculated.' His tone was sharp.

'What if I can't have kids, have you thought about that?'

'We'll cross that bridge when we get there. We're not living in the dark ages. Look at Nikki and Sai.'

'I am not going to get a surrogate or do IVF.'

'Fine, we'll try the natural way, and if we don't fall pregnant I'll accept it. But I want us to at least try to have a family.'

'I thought Zasha and I would be your family. I guess we're not enough.'

'You're twisting my words; you don't get to do that.'

'That's how it's coming across to me.'

'I want to hold a baby too. You got that chance with Zasha, and I deserve one too. Zasha is part of our family, but she's part of Shikhar's too.'

'Dhruv. Her father's name is Dhruv.'

'Sorry, Dhruv, and he will always be her number one man. I want to be the number one man in someone's life too. Is that too much to ask?'

'Nihal, I…I…you're right to want all that, but I can't have another child. It will be hard on Zasha; first, she has to share me with you and then a new baby. Goddamit, she doesn't even know I'm here.'

'You lied to her, again?' Nihal was crestfallen. Eira had done it again. She was hiding their relationship as if she were ashamed of them being together.

'I didn't. I mean, technically I didn't. I will tell her when she's back.'

'Eira, if I'd climbed up to the top as I had decided to and asked you to marry me, would you have said yes?'

'Maybe. We never got to that moment, did we?'

He could tell from the pallor of her face she wasn't expecting to have this conversation.

'You want to say NO.' Nihal scoffed. 'Then why say maybe?'

'Cause I don't know what I would have said or not bloody said.' Eira pounced. He was unnecessarily putting words in her mouth.

'Do you think you have room for anyone else in your life?'

'Nihal, I love me. I've always loved me, but once I had Zasha, I learnt to be less selfish and more selfless. I can't switch hats from mother to lover. I have to be both at all times, and I'm trying. But Zasha is not a grown up. She's far mature for her age, but I can't keep expecting her to be okay with every decision of mine without even consulting her first. Maybe someday I might want another child, and just maybe she will be fine with that. But yes, it is a *maybe*.' Eira tried to reason.

'It's been just you and her for so many years. I think this has more to do with you than with her. You can't accept any change to your family now. Zasha's lucky to have a mom like you, but I don't want to play second fiddle.'

'So, this is it?' Every one of her muscles tensed in her body as she waited for his response.

'I guess.' Nihal's voice echoed his disappointment. 'Think about it. You would have dumped me three weeks from now anyway. Zasha will be back, and she'll flip out when she hears you spent the weekend with my family, and then you'd call me to say *I'm sorry*. So, you take your time and think about it as long as you need to. But for now, I need some space.'

'Nihal, I'm torn, and I wish you could see that. But I also do understand how you feel, and you deserve every bit of happiness.' Eira blinked back the tears, trying hard not to make a public scene.

Nihal held up his hand asking her to stop from saying anything further. He'd heard the "It's not you, it's me…and I want you to be happy" dialogue before. 'I'm going to tell my parents that I got called by the Head of Surgery for an emergency at the hospital. We can leave tonight.'

'We're four hours away. Your parents are not stupid. They are doctors too.'

'And they've also been a couple for 42 years. You are right, they are smart people and will join the dots on their own without me having to spell it out for them.'

Eira held back her tears; she knew he wouldn't care for what his parents thought of them right now. He was angry with her and probably even felt betrayed as if she had led him on. 'I'll take a taxi back. You don't have to leave because of us.'

'Nah, I want to go back to my place too. Do me a favour and just try to keep the mood light until we leave.' Silence sat plump between them trying its very best to push them apart.

Suma noticed Eira wasn't wearing the engagement ring she had given Nihal. Despite all their effort, the awkwardness between them was visible to everyone, but no one poked.

Chapter Nineteen

'What happened on that trail?' Kanika asked, closing the front door behind her. Nihal left immediately after dropping them off, and no hugs or kisses were involved in his goodbye. A boulder of silence had fallen between them.

'Not now Mummy.' Eira continued walking up the stairs.

'We're doing this now, Eira. I'm not your puppet – talk when you tell me to, stand when you say so. I want to know what's going on. You invited me to join you on this trip to meet Nihal's par—' Kanika heard the bedroom door slam shut before she could complete her sentence. Determined to finish the conversation, she followed her daughter up to her room. Eira was curled up on the bedroom floor in a foetal position.

'Lay off, will you?' Eira screamed.

'Not until I know what happened.'

'I told you yesterday that this was too good to be true. I'm sorry to disappoint you again. We broke up.'

'Why?'

'Nihal was going to propose to me today...on that bloody trail. And I would have said *yes* if he had asked me, but before that he wanted a confirmation that I was open to having a baby with him.'

'So?'

'So, we broke up…' Eira sniffled, '…for now, he needs space he says.'

'Eira, do you even think things through anymore?' Kanika helped her get off the floor. 'What is so wrong with him wanting to have a baby with you?'

'I can't do that. Zasha will hate me if I have another baby. Or rather hate me even more than she already does.' Eira's shoulders sagged with dejection.

'Wasn't Dhruv's wife pregnant when she died? Zasha didn't seem to have any problem then. In fact, she was crushed when she learned there wasn't going to be a baby. So, what made you so confident that she doesn't want a sibling? Are you using her as an excuse?'

'Wow. I don't believe this.' Eira paced the room shaking her head derisively. 'He dumps me because my entire world revolves around my daughter, and now you accuse me of using her as an excuse.'

'I'm trying to understand why you would let this man go. He is good for you…don't you see that?'

'We have Zasha. Why can't he accept her as our only child?'

'Zasha's not his, and while he will try to do his best to love her, he knows he will always be competing with Dhruv. Why would anyone want that? Would you?'

'Dhruv's miles away and —'

'Eira, look at how far Nikki has gone trying to have a baby of her own. Most people who want to start a family will at least try to make a baby with the one they love.'

'He should have told me at the very beginning that a child is a deal breaker.'

'Sweetie, you didn't either.'

'What if down the line it didn't work out between Nihal and me, I don't want to have children from two different fathers.'

'Eira, you can't get into a relationship assuming it might not work out and then make every other decision after that based on pessimism. No relationship comes with a guarantee.'

'Unlike mine, your life has been pretty straightforward. I know for sure another baby will complicate my life further.'

'You think my life has been straightforward because that's what I let you see.'

'Meaning?'

'Eira, I have kept a secret from you for thirty-four years, and while I tried to bring myself to tell you about it on several occasions, I just couldn't. I accepted that it would probably go down with me to my grave. But you're a mess, and I now believe I have a humongous part to play in it. You don't trust any man completely, and this distrust finds its way back to your own father.' Kanika's heart was now racing; she had finally started a conversation that right until this moment had replayed itself in her head a million times like a broken record.

'That's not true. I was perfectly fine with Shikhar until he decided to reveal his true colours.'

'Eira, you don't know everything.'

'If this is about Dad and you not wanting children and him refusing to participate in my life...I heard it all at that taash party when *kaki* got drunk. Dad was always indifferent towards me, but I'm past that Mummy. I despised both of you for a long *long* time. I hated how Brinda *kaki* insinuated that I was a mistake. But I also watched you do your very best, and now that I have to be both a mother and father to Zasha, I know it was pretty tough on you.'

'I don't know which taash party you are referring to, but that is not the whole truth. At one point your father and I had agreed we would not have kids. I was happy being the first person in my family to have gone to work, and I was proud of my independence. Back in the day, working with the UN was a matter of pride. It still is, but it was a once-in-a-lifetime opportunity in my time. Your dad, of course, was married to his art. But then five years into our marriage I changed my mind. My biological clock began ticking ferociously, and when I discussed it a few times, he refused. I was at my lowest, and I was having a really hard time trying to accept that I would never be able to enjoy motherhood. But I loved your father too, and I didn't want to leave him.'

'Mummy, where are you going with this?'

'I slipped, Eira. I went against my better judgement.' With that one sentence, Kanika knew she was opening a can of worms, but she had to do it before it was too late.

And then the penny dropped. 'What did you do, Mummy?' Eira mustered the courage to dig deeper.

Kanika's voice dropped to a whisper. 'You're not his biological daughter.'

Eira was jolted into silence; the truth crashing onto her like a fast-moving rock avalanche.

'I had an affair, and I got pregnant. It lasted about a month, I promise, and the moment I got to know I was pregnant, I ended it.'

'So thiiis is what makes us alike?' Her face went blank. 'The fact that we both made mistakes and had children out of wedlock, and I should learn from your mistakes?'

'No. I told you because I see you losing a good man because of something similar.'

'How is this similar? I'm not a liar, and I didn't cheat. Nihal tried to push me to the wall, and when he realized I wouldn't budge, he took to his heels.'

'Eira, I'm sorry.' Kanika felt an acute pang of humiliation and guilt grip her insides.

'No, you don't get to say sorry, and it doesn't make anything alright. Did Dad know I wasn't his child?' Eira asked, her confusion edged with anger.

'No. I never told him. I loved him and didn't want to lose him... or you.'

'So, you let the man believe I was his and now he's dead, so he'll never know.'

'Sometimes you don't have a choice, Eira.'

'There is always a choice...*always*. I crossed the Rubicon too, Mummy. I made some tough choices, difficult ones, and I live with my decisions every day. Don't you tell me that you didn't have a choice. You had *thirty-four* years to tell me he wasn't my father, thirty-four lousy years, and you kept quiet all this time.' Eira's voice quaked with rage.

'And now you think I'm broken because of it...I'm damaged goods, and so you finally picked up the courage to tell me that I am not who I thought I was.' Eira shot back. 'Is my real father alive?'

'I...' Kanika faltered.

'Forget it. I don't want to know.'

'He died of cancer nearly twenty-years ago.'

'Great, so I may be a candidate for cancer in the future.'

'I am truly sorry, Eira. I should have told you a long time ago, and while the world might think I did a horrible thing, I don't regret having that affair. It gave me *you*, the person I love the most in the world.'

'So, I'm your favourite mistake!' Eira recoiled with rage.

'No. The only truth I know is that I wanted to have a child and that I love you so very much. Once I had you, I never ever looked back. You were my whole life. You are my whole life.'

'Enough Mummy. I'm getting grossed out by you justifying an

affair. Please leave. I'd like to be alone for some time.' Eira's eyes misted; memories of the only father she knew came flooding back. She sat sifting through the detritus of all the broken relationships in her life. The rumination continued well into the night.

On Monday, the day limped forward, and with each passing hour, she was getting a little more restless. Eira confined herself to the walls of her bedroom barring the trips to the kitchen for some food. Alice had called several times to check if she was still going to Gina's 4th of July shindig, but Eira ignored all her voice messages. The long weekend was turning out to be a nightmare. By evening she had surrounded herself in filth: an empty ice-cream tub perched on the far end of her bedside table, a pile of dirty clothes from their weekend trip lay at the foot of her bed, and then she saw fruit flies making merry over the pizza corners. From her viewing seat, her life and room had one thing in common: they were both a colossal mess. She was suffering from relationship mourning sickness. Eira finally turned the water on and crawled back into bed waiting for the bathtub to fill up. She couldn't decide what was harder for her to accept: ending the best relationship she'd ever been in or knowing that her entire life had been one jumbo lie. Eira stripped out of her travel clothes and lowered herself in the warm water. She immersed in it all the way to her neck. A few minutes later, she began to scrub violently at her hands, trying to rub off the fake identity she had been wearing all along.

This was crippling.

Of all the setbacks in her life, her mother's confession was the one that tore into her core.

This was a crippling blow to what was left of her morale.

Somewhere in her heart, she'd believed Nihal would call and say he'd changed his mind. That he didn't care if they had children or not, and that all he needed was her: she was enough. But there was stone cold silence at his end. He had locked her out. Eira began to slowly buckle under the weight of her displaced hopes.

On Wednesday, Eira called in sick. She needed a little more time to lick her wounds. That afternoon as she stood by the electric cooking range watching the pasta cook in boiling water, Kanika sat on the kitchen stool in silence waiting for Eira to say something, just anything.

'Do you need something?' Eira's tone was icy.

'Yes. I need you to talk to me...be mad at me...or just tell me what you're thinking.'

'So that you can feel better?'

'Eira we live in the same home. We can't not talk to each other. I know you have many questions, and I'm ready to answer all of them.'

'There's no point in asking you anything. My fathers are dead, who's going to validate what you tell me? For all I know, you will lie all over again to justify your actions.' Any way you sliced it, Eira's words were hurtful and cruel. 'And as for living in the same home, if you're uncomfortable with my silence, you can leave.'

'Leave?' Kanika's legs gave way beneath her.

'I don't have the energy or interest to hear your story. I hate you right now, and I won't forgive you for what you did to me. So, if you're seeking redemption, you're looking in the wrong place. If my indifference is stifling you...leave.'

Eira plucked a spoon from the dishwashing rack and poured the white sauce over the piping hot penne. 'I'm not going to feel guilty about you being there for me when I was pregnant with Zasha. Your support now seems like a cover-up for your own deeds,' Eira declared.

'I'm not going to leave. I don't bail when things get tough. I didn't do it then, and I won't do it now. I won't quit on us. I didn't support you as a cover-up, don't be so harsh. Eira, motherhood doesn't come with an expiry date – valid until it gets challenging. I love you, and I'm going to give you as much time as you need to help us get through this, and we will. I will stay at Fanny's home for a few weeks or until you're ready to have a real conversation and hear my side too.'

'You do what you have to do, Mummy.' Eira poked at a piece of chicken nonchalantly and took a bite.

'Take care of yourself.'

Eira remained seated like a plank.

All by herself in her home, Eira pottered around the house bypassing Kanika's room, trying to make sense of her feelings. Did she feel cheated? Angry? Defeated?

Defeated. That's how she felt. Defeated in love and defeated in life by the people she trusted. The silence in her home was deafening so she switched on the television for some background noise and stared blankly at the screen. A few minutes later, she turned off the TV in disgust and found herself all alone in her home. The man she loved had said goodbye, her mother was gone, and Zasha had chosen her father over her. A long walk usually helped her clear her thoughts or in this situation would at least give her a clue about the next step she had to take. So, she grabbed her car keys and drove to Gravelly Point Park, a place she often visited when she needed some perspective. Lying on the grass and looking up at the sky watching airplanes flying low overhead as they approached Reagan National Airport always gave her an indescribable thrill. When they'd arrived in the capital, Zasha and she would often come down here for a picnic; they would pack a lunch and bring their bikes to ride along the Potomac River. Summertime, the park was crowded with families. Today, there were children everywhere, playing soccer, throwing a frisbee, and couples holding hands while walking their dogs in the middle of the day. And here she was all alone. Her heart hurt with a pain similar to the pricks of cactus quills.

Eira turned her attention away from the perfect lives of these complete strangers and began to walk around the park, followed by a short run before easing herself into a light jog. Her heart was pounding, and she almost dialled Nihal's number. What was the point? Nothing had changed since that last acrimonious confrontation, and yet everything had changed.

After guzzling two bottles of wine, Eira somehow managed to wake up without a hangover the next morning. She consulted her watch; she was up on time for work. The last three days she had been in a funk, but Eira was determined to move forward, as if her break up and her mother's confession had not affected her at all. She couldn't afford to slack off at work; it was the one thing that was holding her together. Alice didn't notice anything different in her behaviour. It was business as usual. Eira left work on time, and when she got home she busied herself with laundry and cleaning up the weekend mess. The next few days continued in a similar fashion; she had no sense of the day of the week and operated like a robot trying to keep up a cool facade before the world. But on Thursday, she cracked and had a mini episode at work. Luckily, Alice was the only one in the restroom. That evening, Eira drove to the hospital and sat outside on the bench just so she could be in the same breathing zone as Nihal. A tiny part of her hoped that she would bump into him or at least see him from a distance, neither of which happened.

When she went back home, she found a shoe box left on the doorstep. Nihal had dropped off some of her things: her toothbrush, a pair of PJs, real-estate brochures, and Kanika's sunglasses that she'd left behind in his car. With this box, he had begun the decathecting process.

'Freakin hell. If I had only stayed home and not gone to the hospital. Shit. *Shit.*' Eira kicked the box into a bed of tulips and sat down on the steps holding her head in her hands. 'I could have seen him, or we could…and now he's gone, leaving me with this box.' She knew that it was going to happen eventually. He would cut her off. But this *this* was a bit premature. Eira was having difficulty breathing, her face was flaming up and her skin prickled. It was a second panic attack in one day. Nihal had literally boxed her out of his life that day.

Chapter Twenty

'*Mia, I've had the best two weeks of my life. I can't wait to tell you all about it in person, but that would mean I would have left India by then.*' Dhruv overheard Zasha gushing over the phone during one of her video chat sessions. He was relieved to know his daughter wasn't homesick or having a hard time adjusting to the city and the Kapur clan.

Nikki flew back to the US that weekend, and while Zasha loved having her around, she knew well enough that her aunt was Eira's eyes and ears. With Dhruv at work and Nikki no longer in the city, she didn't have to worry about the duration of her phone calls to Ari. Their friendship had picked up momentum and was now whirling at top speed: Ari had asked her out to a movie, and no one else was invited. It would be just the two of them, something like a date. At first, Zasha declined. It was too much of a risk. She didn't know how Dhruv would react if she told him the truth and talking to her mother about her blossoming romance wasn't an option either. But then Ari had been so good to her she couldn't think of any reason not to go out with him. So, she succumbed to his undeniably charming ways.

'Hey, you.' Ari pulled out two tickets stubs from the front pocket of his denim shirt and handed one to Zasha. He'd ditched his shorts and flip-flops look for a clean pair of jeans and sneakers. The first thing she'd noticed was that unlike the boys in her school who emptied bottles of hair gel on their head, he didn't use any hair products.

'Popcorn?' Ari affectionately patted the edge of her nose.

'No, I just had breakfast.' Zasha fiddled with the zipper of her bag that had a loose thread stuck in it. 'I've never been to a matinee before.'

'Wow. Then I'm glad I get to take you to your first.'

Zasha looked up from her bag and smiled. 'How much do I owe you?'

'For what?'

'The tickets, duh.' Zasha succeeded at freeing the zipper and plucked out her purple wallet from her bag.

'Is this your first date?' Ari wore a confused smile.

'Why, is this your tenth?'

'Let's say it isn't my first, and this movie is on me.' Zasha wasn't pleased with the way their date had begun. How many girls had he taken to a matinee? Ari was two years older than her, but did he have to put it like that?

They had just settled down in their corner seats when Ari tugged at her hand to get up for the National Anthem. Ten other movie patrons wearing serious faces stared at the screen as the anthem played along. Zasha expected a Spider-Man movie to be a crowd-puller, but then again it was 9.30 a.m. on a weekday. And then somewhere between Peter Parker returning to his high school life and asking Liz to their homecoming dance, Zasha felt five warm fingers reach out for her cold hand. She didn't move. Ari's hand lay light on hers for ten seconds before he slowly let the entire weight rest down and entwined his fingers with hers. She was suddenly conscious of the proximity and promptly looked away from the screen. Zasha felt her hand move up involuntarily. Ari began to kiss it, soft and tender, while his eyes were still glued to the screen as if kissing her hand was part of the whole movie going experience. Mia had cautioned her that he would try to hold her hand, and if he was brave enough, he wouldn't shy away from kissing her.

Oh no. No. *Nu-no.* Zasha panicked. Her heart pumped like a Grand Prix circuit. He was going to kiss her, but she wasn't ready for her first kiss.

Not with Ari.

Not like this in front of so many people, even if it was dark, there were others in the same hall.

Ari slid down lower in his seat, so their faces were at the same height. Zasha flinched as his breath drew closer to her cheek, and then he kissed the edge of her mouth.

'I can't.' Zasha jumped up, spilling Cola all over the seat, a few drops fell on his white sneakers too. 'Sorry...I ...I can't.'

'What the Fu...!' Ari hissed. But Zasha didn't wait, she jumped across him and ran out of the movie hall nearly tumbling over the steps in the dark.

'Did you see a girl run out?' Ari asked the usher at the door, dabbing the cola stains off his jeans and sneakers. The usher pointed to the ladies restrooms.

Fifteen minutes later, Zasha emerged from the restroom hoping Ari had left. But he was standing outside with his arms crossed across his chest.

'Why did you do that? Did I force you to go on a date with me?' Ari's voice was sharp. 'I'm standing here only because of Nikhil. If you were anyone else, I would have gone by now.'

'I don't know what happened to me back there, can we start all over again? It's barely been two weeks...this is too fast.'

'That was first base!'

'Can you keep your voice down? People are staring at us.'

'You're a silly twelve-year-old, who can't handle the fact that teenage life is just around the corner. You want to be treated like a grown-up, but you're not up for it. Let's go. I don't know what I was thinking when I asked you out.'

'I'll tell you what you were thinking…you were thinking with your dick, you prick. How's that for rhyming words?'

'You're no saint yourself. Don't be a prude. You knew what a date meant, and you still chose to come out with me. So, stop playing the victim card, and yea, while I'm a prick, you're a sad ass liar.' Ari glowered. 'I should have listened to Nikhil, but I thought I'd give you a chance to come clean with me when we went for lunch. But no, you have to create a scene for nothing.'

'What did Nikhil tell you?' Zasha was flummoxed. The boys had discussed her. What could he have shared in casual confidence?

'He said you were trouble, just like your mother…and that you lied about your parents being divorced. They were never married supposedly. Your mother has had a few boyfriends, I hear. I thought you were cool like her and wouldn't create a fuss about first base. You're a prude. Don't bother coming by the pool in the evening, go play *doll house* with Khushi.'

Zasha was shocked into stillness. She had no defence. Her silence was an admission of her guilt. She did make up a story about her parent's situation. For a few days there, she had flirted with the idea of belonging to a less dysfunctional family. He was right, she was a liar. And her mother did have boyfriends, but that was none of his business, and more importantly, it wasn't Nikhil's business to talk about her, behind her back. Zasha was livid; first, at herself for lying to a boy just so he would think she led a normal life, and second, at Nikhil for being a lowlife tell-tale. However, an hour later, she regretted lashing out at Ari like that…most of the girls in her school were kissing boys, some were kissing girls too. Mia included.

It had to be her mother's voice in her head that wasn't letting her take the next step. *You have your whole life ahead of you...for boys and sex. Don't let these things distract you from your school work.* There was truth to that wisdom, and so she didn't bother going out with boys from her school. But Ari was different. He was smart, and kind (if she deleted the earlier scene) and he had ignored Nikhil's stupidity and gone out with her. He said he wanted to hear the truth from her... she had indeed overreacted. Zasha dialled his number three times, in an unbecoming act of despair, but he did not respond. She sent him a few messages apologizing for her behaviour. He replied to one of them saying there was no point in taking it further because she was going back in a few days. He invited her back to hang with them at the pool, but she knew he was just being polite.

Later that evening when Dhruv got home from work, he noticed that Zasha hadn't eaten lunch; the dishes were left untouched on the table. The lights in her room were out, and she was sitting on the bed in the dark staring outside her window.

'Honey, are you okay?' Dhruv switched on the table lamp. 'How was your day?'

'Oh, hi Dad. I didn't hear you come in. My day was fantastic.' Zasha's false note of cheer didn't stick.

'Your eyes are puffy.' Dhruv picked up the pillows that were lying on the floor and sat down beside her.

'I think I'm coming down with the flu,' Zasha lied.

'Have you been crying? Did Daadi say something to you?' Dhruv asked firmly.

'I haven't seen Daadi all day.'

'So, what caused all this?' Dhruv pointed to the dirty tissues lying on the floor.

'Daddy,' Zasha threw her arms around him and began to weep. 'Please don't be angry with me. I'm sorry. I...I...I didn't mean to lie.' Zasha choked.

She was going to tell him all about Ari before Nikhil opened his big mouth.

'Honey, let me get you some water. We can talk later.'

'No Daddy. I don't want anything. I wasn't at the mall with a friend today. I don't have any friend from my old school in New York visiting her grandparents here. I lied.' Zasha's voice was shaky. She wiped her face with the back of her sleeves. 'I went for a movie with a boy today.'

'Why are you crying? What did he do to you?' Dhruv's eyes widened. 'Did he hurt you?'

'No. He didn't do anything. I did. I lied to him about you and Mom. I didn't want him to think our family is weird, but he found out, and now he hates me and won't talk to me.'

'Who is this boy? Do I know him?'

'He's Nikhil's friend. His name is Ari.'

Suddenly it dawned on Dhruv; this boy was the source of his daughter's laughter and cheer, and now her pain. Ari was her first crush, and she was hurting. But this wasn't like cajoling her when she was a toddler with a grazed elbow from falling off her tricycle. He couldn't blow gently over the bruise and stick a Mickey Mouse Band-Aid on it reassuring her it would get better in a few minutes. This was his little girl's heart. Dhruv didn't know the protocol for first heartbreak. Should he let her cry it out or should he take her out for icecream to divert her attention away from this boy? Eira would know what to do. She always did. But this was his chance to be both her parent and friend, someone she could trust and always turn to. And so, he sat with her and listened to everything she had bottled up inside her. He may not have known the right words to alleviate the pain, but he knew just how she felt. He'd been hurt too. He was familiar with unrequited affection. The first heartbreak was always the toughest.

'Daddy, I know you think I'm silly because it was just one date.

But I really like him, and I feel pathetic about lying to him.'

'Honey, your sadness is legitimate. There is no hierarchy for heartache. The heart is a funny organ, while it does pump blood to the rest of the body and is pretty much more important than the brain to be alive, it is also the weakest. It flips out when there is the slightest danger of us falling in love. We talk differently; we act differently. Now I don't know what triggered you to have a blowout at the movie hall, and I won't force you to tell me, but I want you to know that I am not angry with you. Am I surprised? For sure. You're my little girl, and it's disturbing for me to see you crying over a boy, but I'm glad we talked.' Dhruv handed her a box of face tissues; Zasha's sleeves were now soaked with her tears.

'Zasha has your mother had the talk with you…about boys and their…?'

'Don't be embarrassing, Dad.'

'Umm, we crossed the embarrassing junction twenty minutes ago.' They dissolved into giggles. Dhruv was pleased to see his daughter smiling.

'I never thought I'd have such strong feelings for a boy I barely know. I've seen girls cry over breakups at school and always thought they were so lame. Then I saw Mom do stupider things like serving her heart out on a platter to a man, only so he could have a stab at it all over again. I'm never going to let myself be so vulnerable again.'

'Honey, you will surely fall in love again, and there is a reasonably high possibility you might be the one calling it quits. This damn heart…' Dhruv tapped the left side of her chest, '… does its own thing and then sometimes we try to force our brain to decide for us. I've never seen the heart and brain agree on the same thing. One always compromises and then we live with those decisions. Eira once tried making a decision with her brain, and that decision caused me a lot of heartache, but her decision also gave me the opportunity to meet the two loves of my life: my wife and you.'

'Are you implying something, Dad?'

'Zasha, you should use this as a teachable moment. We don't choose to fall in love. It just happens, and before you know it, it's taken over your life. Your mother is human; she works like a robot trying to keep everything together, but she does have emotions. Nihal may just be the love of her life. Give it a think, if you can. It might make sense to you.'

'Are you going to tell Mom about this?'

'I expect you to do that...it's your story to tell. But don't take forever or she will kill me if she finds out from someone else.' Dhruv took her by the arm and led her towards the bathroom. 'Go freshen up, and then let's eat together.'

Zasha shut the bathroom door behind her and stared at her reflection in the mirror. Her eyes were swollen, and her cheeks were stained with tears. Her reflection suddenly reminded her of the look on her mother's face when Shikhar and she broke up. Had she given her mother unnecessary grief over and above all that she had already been through? Had she been unreasonable? Was Nihal the love of her mother's life? And was she prepared to find out?

Chapter Twenty-One

15 July 2017

Washington, D.C., USA

7:58 a.m.

'What are you doing here?' Eira asked, rubbing the corner of her bloodshot eyes. The right side of her face had pillow creases and her breath smelt like stale beer.

'You went AWOL on me. Why aren't you taking my calls? I called your mother, and she didn't respond either. I checked with Zasha if you were in touch and she said yes,' Nikki said, her eyes cruising along the mount of filth collected in Eira's living room. 'What the hell happened here? Why is your home like a chicken coop? Where's Kanika aunty?'

'Don't know. Don't care.'

'Excuse me?' Nikki's expression altered. 'Are you still drunk?'

'I may have to stay drunk for the rest of my life if I want to stay sane.' Eira picked up her bra that was lying on the carpet and threw it on the couch.

'Eira, I have a flight to take this evening, so please quit the code.'

'This time my life's hit rock bottom, and it has nothing to do with my poor choices. The last two weeks have been a nightmare. Nihal and I broke up, and as if that wasn't enough, my mother hurled her baggage at me at the same time.'

'Broke up? But…weren't you going to meet his parents?'

'Oh, yea. They're lovely people, and they couldn't wait to plan our wedding.' Eira recalled the conversation she had with Nihal on that hiking trail. 'But their son had one clause, he wanted to negotiate having another child to sign the deal. Surprise. *Surprise*. No baby. NO wedding.'

'And you don't want another child?' Nikki sounded surprised.

'No. Your life is not your own when you have a child. You can try to claim it back every now and then in bits and pieces, but it is never yours completely. I know my daughter; Zasha won't accept it.'

'Zasha refused to accept Nihal, but you continued to be in a relationship with him! Besides, when we were in Mumbai together she was thrilled about the idea of having cousins. She told me she always wanted a sibling.'

'That's different.'

'Explain *how*?'

'The upshot of all this is that we're not together, and I'm right where I was thirteen years ago. Alone, and not any wiser.'

'Eira, I think you've made a *big* mistake. You need to re-evaluate your—'

'My mother has a monopoly over big mistakes. She took over from me. No, actually, she was always the Queen of mistakes. It turns out I'm not Mr Dey's child. The man I thought was my father, was certainly her husband, but I'm the product of an affair she had. She was so desperate for a child that it didn't matter who the father was. That was her justification.' Eira wrestled with the garbage bag that was overflowing with empty beer cans. 'I see no similarity in our situations, so I don't know what triggered her conscience suddenly after keeping the truth from me for thirty-four years.' Eira continued, rancour in her speech. 'Maybe she thought I was already numb with pain; her truth wouldn't hurt as much. Her mea culpa sounded fake. Wait, she felt guilty for messing me up. I have Daddy issues and all that…it's the bloody guilt that was eating her up inside.'

'Where's your mum, Eira?'

'She left…well, technically not left. She's staying with Fanny until I'm comfortable or whatever word she used.'

'Holy God.' Nikki clapped her hand over her mouth. 'And you are okay with her leaving?'

'She'll come back eventually.'

'Eira this is your mother you are talking about. The woman who didn't abandon you when she found out she was pregnant with you, who took you in when you got pregnant with Zasha and has been your constant support through all that life has tossed your way.'

'It was a cover-up.'

'A cover-up for your mistakes? So, you would have appreciated her disowning you instead?'

'Where do you get off, talking to me like that? I'm not the one who cheated and then lied.' Eira retorted, sensing judgement in her friend's voice. 'I've made mistakes, but I didn't hide them so that the world thought I was a saint. She's just selfish.'

'Our time is different. Her situation was different. You had her unconditional support. My support. Dhruv has always been there like a rock you pretend doesn't exist. And now Nihal wants to be there, and you threw him away just because his plans are different from yours and you don't have it in you to alter yours just a tiny bit.'

'Oh, I altered my plans thirteen years ago, and I altered them once again when Shikhar pissed all over me. I'm freakin done. No more. Not for Nihal and certainly not for her.'

'Her…that *her* is your mother. What's got into you?'

'What she has done is unforgivable. I spent years wondering why my father and I had such a distant relationship. Why he never cared enough to spend time with me without having to beg and plead, or be happy for me when I got into an Ivy League school. Nothing I did was good enough to bring a smile to his lips. I had to grow up with that sick feeling in my gut. She said he didn't know I wasn't his… maybe he did. Maybe he saw another man's face in me…and resented me with every fibre of his being. Thanks to him, I've never ever felt good enough. I know she's always been there, but she also took away an equal amount from me. My real father's dead, and I will never get to meet him. Imagine if I had done that to Zasha.'

'Eira, I understand the timing isn't perfect with all that's going on with Nihal and your mom, but I think in a way it is also the best time for you to pick on the demons inside your own head. We can't blame our parents all our lives for who we become. While Zasha may have inherited your crazy temper, she also has her own wandering mind that will lead her to make a fresh batch of her own mistakes.'

'Easy for you to say, Nikki. Your life's perfect.'

'You know what, you're not all that different from Kanika aunty. You are pretty selfish. Come to think of it you've always been self-absorbed, talking about yourself and all your problems. When was the last time you took real interest in my life? If you're unhappy today that's on you, because barring Shikhar, all the other people in your life have always been there for you. You need a good reality check with where you're going with that entitled attitude of yours.'

'Did you come here to lecture me about how pitiful my life is?'

'No. I came to check on you and see if you were fine. That's what friends do. Turns out you are more than fine. So, I'm leaving, and when you can get your head out of your ass, give me a call. I'm at the same number.' Nikki slammed the front door shut.

'Great. Now my best friend hates me too. Well done.' Eira sank back into the rocking chair feeling emotionally naked. She shut her eyes tight wishing all of it would go away: the hurt, the pain, the deceit, and the love that she still had for Nihal too.

By mid-noon, Eira had rewound the conversation she had with Nikki that morning for the umpteenth time. Now she had to clear the thoughts that clouded her mind to listen to what her heart had to say. She decided to take a brisk walk around her block, but that somehow turned into a grocery shopping trip. A couple of hours later, she returned with bags topped with fruits and crunchy vegetables. Eira threw away the rest of the cheesy corn chips and emptied out the remnants of chocolate bars and ice-cream tubs from her fridge. She eased into her couch with a tall creamy strawberry and blueberry smoothie, when her phone began to vibrate. She recognized the number. It was the George Washington University Hospital board line. Nihal had finally come to his senses and was calling to apologize.

'Hi, I'm Betty, and I'm calling from George Washington University Hospital. Am I speaking with Ms Eira Dey?'

'Yes. This is Eira. What is this regarding?'

'Your number is mentioned as an emergency contact for Mrs Kanika Dey on her medical card that we found in her wallet. We tried calling earlier and left a voice message too.'

'What's going on? Where is my mother?' Colour drained from Eira's face. She was like a deer caught in the headlights.

'Your mother and her friend Ms Nikki Kapur have been in an accident and are currently being treated at our hospital. You need to come to the hospital right away.' Betty intoned gravely.

'But my mother doesn't drive. How did this happen?' Eira could feel her stomach rise up to her throat.

'Ms Dey, the officers are investigating the case. All I know is that a car lost control on the corner of 24th street and Pennsylvania Avenue, and crashed into a café killing three people on the spot and injuring seven others.'

"Car crash," those two words conjured up several grisly images in Eira's mind. Would her mother survive or be rendered brain dead? Will Nikki be able to walk again? What if one of them fell into a coma or worse still a vegetative state. The hairs on her arm prickled and fear invaded her chest.

Breathe, Eira. You've got this.

They are alive, and they're going to be fine.

They have to be fine.

Breathe.

Eira's hands trembled as she began to collect her mother's past medical charts and insurance papers. Her brain was numb, and she found it hard to locate any of the documents. Eira flopped down on the floor and held her face in her hand, knees bunched under her wet chin when suddenly she heard a phone bleep. It wasn't hers, because that was in her pocket. Her eyes followed the sound of the incoming message beeps and stopped at a silver body phone lighting up on her dining table. It was Nikki's phone.

Sai: *Hey baby. The agency called.*

Sai: *The surrogate's reports are all clear.*

Sai: *Call me when you can. Love you.*

Sai didn't know his wife had been taken to the hospital. Eira had to let him know; he would hate her when he came to know who and why Nikki was with at that café. But this was no time to think about being on his good side. Eira grabbed her purse and left for the hospital hoping to find her mother and best friend with mild bruises.

Walking into GW University Hospital again after nearly three weeks, Eira realized that bumping into Nihal was no longer her fear. Life had a strange way of helping her deal with her challenges: it replaced the old with the new. Now she had the trepidation of losing her mother, and her best friend, had she been more in control of her emotions, this situation could have been entirely avoided.

Eira stopped by the nurses' station, and they directed her to one of the doctors who had performed the emergency craniotomy on Kanika. He explained to her that the paramedics had brought her mother to the hospital five hours earlier. Kanika's systolic blood pressure was high, and they ordered a CT scan, which showed an epidural hematoma: bleeding and inflammation in the brain that was putting pressure on the skull. Their neuro team had recommended brain surgery to remove the hematoma. Kanika was now in the recovery room, and they were watching her vital signs closely.

Eira was allowed to peep into the recovery room through the glass window through which she saw Kanika lying in bed with her eyes closed. Her head was bandaged with a gauze dressing, and her frail body was hooked up to multiple monitors, an IV drip, and a thick tube ran through her mouth down her throat. They were now waiting for her to wake up to assess if she responded well to straightforward commands and to check for complications from the surgery. There was a reasonable possibility Kanika could suffer from disabilities caused due to damage to the brain tissues.

Eira then went to visit Nikki who had sustained a few minor injuries herself, but her medical reports were all clear, and she was out of danger.

'I'm sorry, Eira. I am *so* very sorry. I should not have interfered. I shouldn't have gone to see Kanika aunty. It was my stupid idea to take her to that café. I thought she would feel better if she could talk to someone. Fanny isn't someone she talks to. You are her family, and it was you she needed to talk to, not me. I overstepped. I am so sorry.' Nikki was inconsolable. 'I will never forgive myself if anything happens to her.' She cried, echoing Eira's own fear.

'Stop.' Eira shushed her. 'You were only trying to help. You didn't ram your car into that café. It was a freak accident. I'm just happy you are okay. I love you heaps, and I am sorry for not being a better friend to you.' Eira reached for Nikki's hand and grasped it tight. 'My mother is a fighter. She'll get through it. I just know it. Ma, is resilient. *That's what makes us alike, our fighting spirit, not the mistakes.* We're all fallible, but only a few have the courage to accept their mistakes and do their best to make it right. You'll see, she'll bounce back. She has to. I haven't let her off the hook. I won't let her die on me like this. We were finally talking…communicating. I have a bone to pick with her. There's so much I need to say to her…so much to know from her…and tons to learn. Like a *Kintsugi* crafter, she's always helped me find the gold in my flaws, helping me deal with my brokenness. She's my person, my fortress, and I didn't even realize it. All this time, she stood on the side letting me take centre stage, as if I had it all under control. But she held on just a little bit without me knowing, just in case I fall, and I did. Several times. Oh God! *Please.* Please let her be okay. I can't do this…I can't go through life without her, knowing that the last thing I said to her was that I *hate* her.' Eira's jaw tightened, and her chin trembled. Her world was collapsing in slow motion, and there was nothing she could do.

'Ms Dey, your mother has regained consciousness and is being moved to the Neurosurgical ICU. The doctor would like to see you.' The red-head intern monitoring Kanika's progress reported.

'Thank you, God.' Nikki clutched the side of the bed and whispered a silent prayer.

'I've informed Sai and Dhruv, they'll be here soon. I'm going to go check on my mother now. I'll be right back, alright.'

Nikki waved her a tired hand and continued to pray for Kanika.

Chapter Twenty-Two

When Kanika opened her eyes, she felt small and weak in that large hospital bed. The attending surgeon shined a penlight into her eyes to check if her pupils constricted, and they did. He then asked her to squeeze her hands and wiggle her toes. Kanika followed his instructions with comfortable ease.

'She has good reflexes.' The surgeon nodded. 'Mrs Dey, do you know the month of the year?' He proceeded with the questioning. Kanika had passed the first two tests, just one more and they would know for sure if she was in the clear. Her eyes moved slowly across the room, and she saw Eira standing by her bedside along with two other doctors and a nurse. She didn't answer.

'Mrs Dey, you were in an accident and had brain surgery, if you could just try and answer a few questions for us.' The surgeon pressed on. 'Do you remember your home address?'

'Please Mummy, say something.' Eira squeezed her mother's hand. 'Tell them where you live. Tell them you live with me,' Eira begged.

A tear trickled down Kanika's cheek; her daughter's home was still her home too. There was a tiny possibility Eira would forgive her, and they would return to be the way they were.

'July,' Kanika's voice was tired, and her mouth was dry. '…9th Street NW, Washington, D.C,' she said faltering.

'Whoosh. You did it, you remembered, Mummy.' Eira cheered and kissed Kanika's hand. 'That's our home address, Doctor.'

'That's fantastic. The doctors will observe you for one more day in the ICU, Mrs Dey. If all signs point to the positive, you will be moved to the general hospital ward for further nursing care.'

'How many days will she have to be in the hospital?' Eira asked. 'I'm asking because I'm her only caregiver, and I want to be there for her through it all.'

'A week to ten days for sure. It all depends on how well it heals.' The surgeon left the room, and his band of interns followed him out, leaving the nurse to take care of the remaining assessment. Eira was allowed fifteen minutes in the ICU with her mother and was informed she could return later for a second visit. Eira pulled a chair and sat down by her mother's bedside. *I love you Mummy,* is all she said. Kanika needed to hear just that. No long charades of apologies or excuses or reasons. They were happy to be in each other's presence living those quiet moments together. "When you become a mother, every other relationship seems pale in comparison," Kanika had once told her when she was growing up. And it was true, being a mother to Zasha trumped every other relationship in her life. Zasha was right; there was no need for a patchwork family. They had each other, and that's how life had intended for it to be. There was no point fighting the truth.

After two gruelling hours of medical paperwork and police formalities, Eira returned to Nikki's room and saw Sai seated by her side. She waited out for a few minutes and watched Nikki's face beam, while Sai caressed her non-bandaged wrist.

'Hey, Sai.' Eira gave him a peck on the cheek. 'Your wife looks perky.'

'After the news I just gave her…it would be impossible for her not to be perky. Our surrogate's results are in, and it's all good.' Sai was buoyant. 'We might be meeting her early next month. The agency is checking on her availability too.'

'They're all so professional. It's hard to believe a birthing process can be like this too,' Nikki said, trying to sit up on her bed.

'That's a fantastic start. All the very best, love. You two are going to be fantastic parents.'

'Thank you, I finally have my silver lining,' Nikki reckoned. 'You know, I was thinking, had I known I'd never get pregnant I would have enjoyed latex-free sex all those years.' Nikki divulged. The two friends burst into a cachinnation. Nikki was beginning to see the lighter side of her situation and learning to joke about it.

'I'm outta here. You women are crazy.' Sai patted Eira on the back and left the room to meet the doctors about his wife's discharge procedures.

'Have you seen aunty again?' Nikki asked sipping on a glass of water.

'Two visits are all I get. I'll check on her before I go home for the night. Zasha and Dhruv have boarded their flight. They should be here tomorrow afternoon or early evening. I need to make up Mummy's room for Dhruv to sleep in, and you and Sai can take mine. I'll bunk with Zasha.' Eira arched her back with a cracking sound. 'I need coffee. I'm gonna head to the cafeteria and check out the prison-like food they sell.'

'I don't think I will be discharged today. So, I'll see you in the morning.' Nikki reached out for Eira's hand. 'I'm sorry for being a pathetic friend. I should never have reacted the way I did. It was too soon. Too bloody soon. Damn it! I should have been listening to you about Nihal, instead, I lectured you on motherhood. I'm a terrible person. Kanika and you are wonderful mothers. I hope I can be half as lovely with my own.'

'You did the right thing by sounding me off. I needed a dose of reality. On the bright side, this accident did get me out of the dark space that I was slowly spiralling into. Believe me, it was a hollow, depressing place. So, we're good.' Eira lifted Nikki's hand and kissed it. 'Close your eyes. I'll see you in a few hours.'

Eira went down to the cafeteria and strolled passed the food stations trying to decide on what she wanted to eat. She settled on a burrito and a cappuccino.

'Damn, you, stupid shit,' Eira swore at the ketchup dispenser. Something was blocking its output, so she pressed down hard, a little too hard that it made the ketchup spill out of the plastic containers and all over the counter. Murphy's law was in full force. Her day was turning out to be a write-off.

Nihal was standing up ahead picking up an onion and cream cheese bagel and noticed the slamming of the ketchup dispenser. He recognized her voice. Nihal walked up to Eira and offered her a bunch of paper towels to clean up the ketchup that had also splattered on to her sleeve.

'Are you visiting someone?' Nihal asked. It was the safest starter conversation after weeks of no communication.

'My mother is admitted here,' Eira nodded and moved towards the tables.

'What happened?' Nihal pulled out a chair and sat down facing her. It didn't feel as awkward as he'd imagined it would. Eira told him all about the accident and the details she knew about Kanika and Nikki's injuries.

'Why didn't you call me?'

'You are a paediatric surgeon, not a neurosurgeon.' Eira threw her head back in surprise.

'Eira, we're still friends, and I'm a doctor.'

'I didn't know we were still doing the friendship thing. You didn't leave a note in the box you dropped off like a coward at my doorstep.'

Embarrassment surged through him, and he tried to think of the best reason for his actions, but words failed him. 'How can I help now?'

'We're doing fine. Nikki's husband is here.' Eira said, unwrapping the foil around her burrito. 'Actually, there is one thing you can do. Can you help me get a longer visit in the ICU? I was allowed only fifteen minutes earlier.'

'I'll come along and see what I can do. I'll also have a quick chat with her doctor to understand her post-op progress.'

'Thanks. That would be really helpful.' Eira said, slowly easing herself into the conversation. 'I didn't understand some of the medical terms they were using.'

Nihal noticed she was still wearing the earrings he had given her. Did it mean there was still room for a compromise or did she just not care enough to be bothered about things he'd given her? Were they just any other earrings to her? Standing inches away from her in the elevator and taking in the faint smell of her perfume he felt a wave of guilt rush through him. Had he jumped the gun too soon? Did returning her things give him any closure at all or was it just a nasty jab to make her feel guilty. Nihal wanted to push the stop button of the elevator and hold her in his arms and kiss her and tell her how much he still loved her, except that Eira didn't seem the least bit affected by his presence. Maybe she hadn't changed her mind and never would. Or maybe she was just preoccupied with her mother's recovery.

Nihal spoke to the head nurse of the ICU unit and got Eira an additional fifteen minutes with her mother. He had a quick discussion with Kanika's doctor and assured Eira her mother was getting the best treatment that there was, and she would soon be on the road to recovery; however, he did mention that complete rehabilitation would take a month or even more. Secretly, Eira was happy she'd bumped into him. It was good to have someone to talk to at a time like this; nonetheless, she wasn't going to let him know how she felt.

If he had cared about her he would have given her time, then again, he was in a hurry to move on and so he'd returned her things for closure.

Eira spent a restless night in bed. Too many decisions were weighing her down. Should she tell Zasha about the breakup immediately or wait a while? Did Zasha need to know the truth about her grandfather? The realtor had been hounding her for a confirmation too, which meant she had to go on the final house tour with Zasha within the next ten days or lose out on the house she had her eye on for so long. But did she have the bandwidth to change schools and houses along with caring for her mother who had just undergone brain surgery? She was bound to drop a ball. She couldn't do it all. She had to ask for help or put some of the items in her life on hold.

When Eira reached the hospital the next morning, Kanika was awake and much more alert. She had been taken in for another CT scan, and the tube had been taken out of her mouth.

'Nihal was here.' Kanika's voice was hoarse and unclear.

'He probably came to check on you. I bumped into him in the cafeteria last night.' Eira said matter-of-factly without divulging into any more details. 'Anyway, how are you feeling now?'

'Better, I guess. But my head still hurts a little.'

'Have you told the doctor?'

'Yea, he said it was normal after brain surgery. They will relook at my CT scans today and move me to the general patient's ward accordingly. How's Nikki?'

'She's getting discharged today. Sai's here, and he's taking her to our home. They'll stay with us for a bit.' Eira noticed her mother zoning out. Fatigue began to set in, something else the doctors said was normal after surgery. Eira arranged for a private room for her mother and then made a quick trip home to drop off Nikki and Sai. She kept herself busy to avoid even the slightest thought of Nihal from entering her mind. But there he was, standing outside her mother's room, in his scrubs, looking as handsome as he always did. Despite all the chaos surrounding her, every time she stood in his presence, she felt peaceful.

'Mom, Mom.' Zasha yelled across the corridor, and an irate nurse shushed her with a stern glare. Behind her was Dhruv, and going solely by his appearance, it was hard to believe he had just gotten off a twenty-one-hour long flight.

'How's Nani?' Zasha flung her arms around Eira and began to cry. 'How did all this happen?' Zasha asked, disengaging herself. 'I want to meet her.' Zasha hurried towards Kanika's room before Eira could tell her more.

'Zasha was worried crazy on the flight.' Dhruv explained, stroking Eira's cheek with a reassuring touch. 'I'm here. You don't have to worry about anything.' She threw her arms around his waist and broke down. Eira had kept it together for forty-eight hours. She just needed to let it all out. But she had no idea that she was being watched. Dhruv held on to her and caressed her hair gently. It took her a few minutes to compose herself, but when she did Nihal was no longer standing outside her mother's room.

Initially, Nihal was confused by Dhruv's presence in Eira's life, but now the picture was clear. He had seen in first hand. Eira and Dhruv were family first, even if they weren't married. Dhruv was always there for her. They weren't like those estranged couples who couldn't stand to be in the same room with each other. Dhruv was no longer married, maybe he would make a move on Eira again, after all, they had a daughter together, and no one could change that. And he clearly still cared deeply for her. Who wouldn't? Eira was a splendid woman.

Chapter Twenty-Three

Kanika was discharged from the hospital by the thirteenth day. The doctors called her speedy recovery a miracle given her age and the extent of the injuries. Dhruv stayed for the entire duration that Kanika was in the hospital. He knew Eira could do with some support even though she'd never ask. And although Zasha was disturbed by her grandmother's accident, she was also relieved to be home in a familiar surrounding with her family, away from Ari and all their misunderstandings. She had attempted to talk to Eira about Ari, but the timing just seemed awkward. Her mother didn't need the additional stress of a tween daughter who was merely acting on impulse.

Kanika continued to wear a bandana to cover up the patch that they had shaved off for the surgery. In a month's time, her regular appetite had returned, and the mild limp in her right leg had disappeared, regardless of which the doctors asked her to keep her schedule as light as possible. Kanika resumed her book club meetings, but she stepped down from her positions at the Welfare Centre and Green Feet movement. During the initial weeks, she refused to travel by car or any means of public transportation. Fear had stacked up inside her, and she preferred staying indoors. Kanika soon began to visit a counsellor to help her with the nightmares she began to have after the accident. She was having difficulty sleeping too. Kanika's psychological rehabilitation took a lot longer than her physical recovery, but Eira and Zasha were patient with her giving her all the time she needed to put the traumatic near-death experience behind her.

September was a busy month with Eira moving to a new house, and Zasha adjusting to her new school, away from Mia. In the fullness of time, Zasha opened up to her mother about Ari, and to her surprise, her mother wasn't disappointed in her. She, per contra, was proud of the way Zasha had dealt with the situation single-handedly. However, discussions on her tumultuous relationship with Nihal was a no-go zone.

Nihal didn't contact her after that day at the hospital when he'd seen Dhruv and her together, and she never ever bumped into him at any of Kanika's follow up appointments. As far as Eira was concerned, love was a closed chapter in her life. She had had her chance at a real relationship with Dhruv. They could have been a family, and she could have enjoyed a blissful married life minus all the complications, hurt, betrayal, and embarrassment that she had called upon herself. But she'd taken the road less travelled, and now their lives would not meet at an intersection.

'Why won't Mom talk about Dr Zane? What happened between them? Come on, Nikki aunty. You must tell me. Have you seen her lately? She's like a zombie operating on coffee and chocolate. Mom is emotionally paralyzed.' Zasha whispered into the phone on a late October evening. 'She loves Halloween, and we haven't even bought our costumes this year.'

'Do I have to remind you that your Nani and I had a nearly fatal accident not too long ago?'

'You had a few stitches,' Zasha chuckled.

'Not funny, you weren't there.'

'I know. I know.'

'It's been a tough year for her, so stop bugging her about Nihal. She will tell you when she's ready.'

But Nikki's excuses were no longer holding water. 'I can't let it go. I know she misses him because I've heard the crying through her bedroom door. The other day, she was staring at a photo of him on her laptop, and when she realized I may have seen it, she switched windows. She's not over him. Did Mom break up with him because of me? Or was it something else? I feel terrible – I don't want her to be miserable because of me.'

'I'm not a hundred per cent sure, Zasha. She doesn't talk about it…after Kanika aunty's accident, she's begun to keep to herself. I don't know what's really going on in her mind anymore.'

'Tell me what you do know,' Zasha persisted.

'Nihal nearly proposed marriage, but he also told her he wanted to have more children.'

'So?'

'That's what I said too.'

'Dad wanted more kids.'

'Well, she thought you wouldn't be fine with having a sibling and was afraid to lose you. So, she broke up with him. To be fair to her, at that time you were behaving like a prima donna. She didn't know better.' Nikki paused. 'That boy did change you…I should give him some credit for cracking a hard nut.'

'She told you about Ari?'

'I get to know everything, little one. I have my sources.'

'Did your sources also tell you that we're now friends, and it's all in the past?'

'That's very grown up.' Nikki was distracted by a second call that was beeping on her phone. 'Let me call you back. It's Tasha. I don't want to keep her waiting. It could be something urgent.' Tasha was Nikki's surrogate who was now carrying their twin babies.

'Ciao. Talk soon.'

Zasha visited the local mall a weekend before Halloween and picked up a costume for Eira and herself. With some help from Mia, they got the boxes of decorations out and carved a jack-o'-lantern too. Eira appreciated her effort, but there wasn't much change in her enthusiasm.

'Mom, we need to talk. You can't walk around as if you've been struck by lightning. Why did you call it off with Dr Zane?' Zasha's question drew her a blank stare. Eira placed a heavy laundry basket filled with fresh, warm clothes down on the floor waiting for her daughter to elaborate on her assessment.

'I'm still wet behind the ears as far as love is concerned, but I know what it feels to really like someone and to have no control over that feeling. Please get back with Dr Zane. You don't need to live like a monk because of me. I know I gave you shit…apologies for my language…but you know me. I'm always on your side, Ma. I would never be jealous if you decided to have another baby, in fact, I'd love to have a little brother or a sister. I'll even help you take care of them. It's so nice to see Dad and Nikki aunty laughing, arguing and teasing each other. I want that too.'

'I don't know what Nikki's told you, which she shouldn't have in the first place, but that ship has sailed. Nihal doesn't want to be with me, and I didn't give him reason enough to want to stay. I was never sure about anything when we were together. I want him to be happy and to have a family that I can never give him. I have you baby girl.' Eira cupped her daughter's chin 'You are all I need. You are enough for me.' Eira pressed a kiss on Zasha's forehead.

'Mom you'll always have me, but you need to live your life too. You need to have that one big love, just like Dad. All these years you've made your life about me, and I'd be lying if I said I didn't feel a little jealous to share you with Dr Zane. But—'

'Zasha, let me be the mother here. I've made my decision.' Eira clammed up.

'No Mom. It can't end like that. You have to do something about it.' Zasha encouraged. 'Tell me how I can help?'

'Sweetheart, I know I haven't been in the best of moods, but I will get back at my own pace. I'm in no rush to be with a man. Now go on and check on Nani. See if she needs anything.' Eira forced a smile and returned to folding the laundry.

Just after Halloween, much against Mia's advice, Zasha visited Nihal at the hospital. She feigned an emergency and got an appointment with him.

'Can I get you something to drink? Juice…water?' Nihal asked, depositing his stethoscope on the desk.

'No, thanks.' Zasha crossed her feet at the ankle and arched her body forward with purposeful erectness.

'What brings you here today? I'm certain your mother has no clue you are meeting me.' His gaze swivelled from the wall clock to her.

'Don't worry, I didn't cut school. Dr Zane, this will only take up a few minutes of your time. I came here today to apologize for my behaviour. I'm sorry that my mother and you aren't together, and I'm sorry that I gave you'll a hard time, but can you please strike off the past and reconcile with my mom? I promise I won't cause any more trouble. I want my mother to be happy, and you make her happy Dr Zane. Mom has always put me first. She deserves to live her own dreams too.'

Nihal fixed his eyes on her for a minute before answering. 'Zasha, it's—'

'Please don't say it's too late.' Zasha pleaded, her lips pressed into a straight line.

'I'm afraid it is. I've been offered a position to head the paediatric unit at a hospital in New York, and I'm supposed to let them know my decision by the end of this week.'

'So, it's not too late then. Tell them you don't want it.'

'Oh, Zasha. This is a once in a lifetime opportunity. You're still too young to understand how this can be a game changer for me.' Nihal's voice was tight. He wanted to be in control of the conversation.

'That's your call, Dr Zane. I know Mom still loves you. The ball is in your court now. If you change your mind message me.' Zasha scribbled her number and their new home address on a writing pad on his desk. 'I'll save you a seat at our Thanksgiving dinner. If you don't show up, I'll understand. I wish you the best, Dr Zane.' Zasha offered her hand for a handshake, but Nihal patted her on the head instead.

23 November 2017

Thanksgiving Day

Nihal never messaged or called Zasha after their meeting, and nothing could assuage the disappointment she felt at being unable to unite her mother with the man she loved. She confided in her grandmother, but Kanika wasn't very forthcoming with any new ideas. She chose not to interfere in Eira's love life any more. Dhruv had arrived from India a day earlier to spend Thanksgiving with them, and Nikki and Sai flew in that morning. Eira slaved all day in the kitchen trying to put together a traditional American Thanksgiving dinner: roast turkey, cranberry sauce, snowflake potatoes, baked carrots, and fruit cake, and just to spice it up they made chicken *Chettinad* and *jeera* rice too. Before dinner, they went around the table, and each one shared what they were thankful for that year.

'I'm thankful for my babies who are now seven months away from meeting their mommy and daddy, and I'm thankful I'm alive and survived that accident.' Nikki twiddled with the tablecloth. 'But above all, I'm thankful for you guys here around this table: my lovely family.' Nikki's eyes were brimming with heartfelt gratitude.

When it was Zasha's turn to share, she seemed distracted.

'Are you waiting for someone? Why are you staring at the front door?' Eira asked.

'Please don't tell me it's that boy.' Dhruv's eyes popped out.

'No. I'm not expecting anyone.' Zasha held her mother's hand and proceeded to share her gratitude. 'I'm thankful this year for Nani's recovery, my lovely family, our new home, and my new iPhone.'

'You can thank me for your iPhone,' Dhruv winked.

The table lit up with laughter

Sai and Dhruv helped with clearing the table, while the girls enjoyed a second round of fruitcake, this time with a scoop of ice cream. Nikki heard a soft tap on the door, and she turned down the music. She exchanged a surreptitious glance with Zasha and hastily shuffled to the door to see who it was.

'Eira, you have someone at the door for you,' Nikki called out.

'At this hour?' Eira straightened her skirt and sauntered towards the front door. A gust of cold wind chased the orange leaves from their yard through the foyer.

'What are you doing here, Nihal?' Eira asked, perplexed seeing him at the stoop of her house. She grabbed a jacket and stepped out on the porch, shutting the door behind her.

'I honestly don't know. I should be on a plane to New York right now, but an hour ago, I was standing outside the airport desperately searching for a sign that would make me stay back here in D.C., but I couldn't lie to my soul. I was looking for your face in that crowd. And so, I'm here, standing at your doorstep, just as your daughter instructed.'

'Zasha? When did she meet you?'

'She came by the hospital last month, and we had a brief chat. Her child-like honesty made me realize how stupid I've been. I tried to railroad you. I rushed you into meeting my parents with their hideous wedding plans, and then I tried to arm-twist you into making promises about having children, when the truth is, none of it matters to me. I want you in my life Eira. I love you. I never stopped thinking about you. I was quiet but not without the heaviness that I carried around in my heart.'

'Why didn't you ever call me?' Eira's eager eyes looked up at him searching for an answer.

'The night your mother was hospitalized I saw Dhruv with you at the hospital. I could not bear to see another man so involved in your life. I was jealous. I was the outsider, and he was your family.'

'Dhruv will always be family, and that will never change. You said you loved me and then turned on heel when our opinions clashed. You didn't bother to put up a fight and simply gave up on us; whereas Dhruv's been solid all these years despite our differences.' Eira pulled her coat tighter around herself.

'I'm sorry. Please give me a chance to find a way back into your heart.'

'Nihal, I'm work in progress. I'm imperfect and I mess up. Please don't try to fix me. I am not embarrassed of my missteps. My flaws make me who I am. My life doesn't follow a script, never has, never will. Zasha and I won't be trouble-free people to live with. Our life won't be a pocketful of sunshine. If we do this...if we take this next step together, know that I won't stop trying to give my best. I won't be the one who will walk away when the screws tighten on us. It may seem as if I am crumbling or giving up, but I won't until I know that you don't want to try anymore. I'm scared, and I'm terrified, but I want to do this too. So, hold my hand. I'm gonna need it.' Eira felt a lump form in her throat.

'I love you. You and I, this is for real.' Nihal hooked a stray hair behind her ear and kissed her lips. 'This is our life now, and we're going to be a solid team.'

'Tomorrow, at this time…today will be over. Let's give *us* a try again.' Eira crooned, burrowing her face in his jacket, in her little comfort spot as she always did.

ABOUT THE AUTHOR

Donna Dias Manuel grew up in Mumbai, in an estrogen-dominated family. She has a degree in Geology from St. Xavier's, Mumbai and an MBA from Deakin University, Melbourne. After working in media, advertising, and finance in Mumbai, she moved to Bangkok and began her writing journey. Her debut novel, **Love is Never Easy**, was published in 2017. Presently, she lives in Toronto with her husband and daughter.

'**What Makes Us Alike?**' is her second novel.

* 9 7 8 9 3 5 4 3 8 5 7 9 7 *